BEGINNINGS

ROBERT GRIGG

BEGINNINGS

A SHORT STORY TRILOGY

Columbus, Ohio

This book is a work of fiction. The names, characters and events in this book are the products of the author's imagination or are used fictitiously. Any similarity to real persons living or dead is coincidental and not intended by the author.

The views and opinions expressed in this book are solely those of the author and do not reflect the views or opinions of Gatekeeper Press. Gatekeeper Press is not to be held responsible for and expressly disclaims responsibility of the content herein.

Beginnings: A Short Story Trilogy

Published by Gatekeeper Press
2167 Stringtown Rd, Suite 109
Columbus, OH 43123-2989
www.GatekeeperPress.com

Copyright © 2021 by Robert Grigg
All rights reserved. Neither this book, nor any parts within it may be sold or reproduced in any form or by any electronic or mechanical means, including information storage and retrieval systems, without permission in writing from the author. The only exception is by a reviewer, who may quote short excerpts in a review.

iStockphoto.com/Solovyova (boy with bicycle), johnrandallalves (whitetail buck), MilosStankovic (man with dog).

Library of Congress Control Number: 2021934980

ISBN (paperback): 9781662911804
eISBN: 9781662911811

Dedicated to:

James A. Fierens Sr.

And

Dr. John E. Hart

For caring to open a door
When I knocked.

Contents

"Beginnings" 1

"A Boy's Death" 43

"Manhood" 71

"Beginnings"

"I'll become a mystery man. A spy. A stranger from a different land." My eyes began to widen. "Sure enough, that's *just* what I'll do! Why didn't I think of that before?"

I released a heavy sigh. I had nearly given up, almost believing it was impossible after thinking blankly for nearly five minutes about it.

"Yep," I said quietly. "That's all I have to do. Why, I'll even change my name when I disappear, and then no one will know who I am. That'll keep me from getting caught – cause if they knew my *real* name, they'd haul me back here, and then Dad would whomp on me for sure!"

Overhead, the boards creaked to the pressure of my mother's feet as she walked across the upstairs living room floor. I resumed my breathing, feeling once again safe and secure in the darkness of the dimly lit basement.

The plan nearly complete, my eyebrows lowered as I squinted and gathered some socks and a pair of jeans and packed them neatly into the paper grocery bag. My hooded sweatshirt and a lightweight jacket were already folded, so I quickly placed them in as well.

"Hmm, let's see…" I sat on the old-smelling couch, the one I loved to slap with my hand and watch the dust fly from. I chewed at my lower lip and scratched the stubble of blond hair behind my ear.

"Gee's. Now that I'm going to change my name, what do I call myself?" I stared into the darkest part of the basement. "Hmm…. my best friend was Mark. I don't want to use his name and get him into trouble. And then there's…." My face brightened. "Why sure! That no-good Nick. If I do something wrong, he'll get the blame for it. That'd teach him to borrow everything from me and forget to bring it back. Maybe if Mark heard about the bad things Nick did, he'd want me back as a friend again, too." I lowered my head and returned to my packing. "That's what it'll be!" I said decisively. "I'll call myself Nick Findley. No one will know who I am now!"

The basement was cool and damp; even when my Mom occasionally came down to start another load of wash, she didn't know I was there. I was working rapidly but was careful not to hit against the paper bag; the sound of which would have even perked up a cat's ears. I placed the last of my stuff neatly into it – a toothbrush, a glass jar containing $6.67, a two-piece fishing pole, and my most prized possession – a baseball hat, the one I had gotten for playing third base on the Minor League team. I carefully tried to roll the end of the bag up so nothing could fall out, then leaving it on the couch, snuck quietly upstairs.

I could feel the heat hit my face as I silently reached the top of the steps. Without stopping, I carefully opened the backdoor and stepped outside. A pearl-white sun blazed from a cloudless, hazy sky as I quickly sought the cool shade of the old hangout – beneath the big oak tree in the backyard. I sat down and leaned up against the main trunk, just like my old buddies and I used to do. I sighed. Used to do – now they had other friends or always something else to keep busy with. But never with me.

"I'm just too ugly." I grumbled to myself. "I wear the wrong clothes. And I always say the wrong thing. They don't even like the candy I buy them." I plopped my chin on the palms of my hands and stared at the ground. The familiar silence surrounded me until an irritating buzz of a mosquito hovered near the side of my head. I swatted with my hand and slapped my face hard. The silence returned.

Suddenly a tiny dog squeezed beneath the backyard fence and bounded over to me. I smiled and began to laugh as I saw him out of the corner of my eye. The clumsy little beagle seemed to be running as hard as he could, but at any moment, looked as if he would fall forward and skid his little black nose onto the grass. I greeted him with caresses and set him on my lap as his tail wagged like a pendulum gone haywire.

"Where'd you come from little fella? Hah? You're not even wearing a dog tag or collar."

He was licking my hands and arms, then gave me a kiss on the side of my face.

I laughed and hugged him. "You sure are a cute little guy. You're so friendly. I wish I could …" But then I felt the distraction. "Nope… It's no good. I *can't* take you with me. I sure wish – golly gee, you don't know how I'd like to – but you'll have to stay here." I placed him on the grass in front of me and pointed a finger at him. Scoldingly I said, "Stay".

The dog responded by climbing back onto my lap, his tail and tongue moving so fast that you could hardly tell them apart.

But I had my mind set. Not even a puppy-dog was going to stop me. I had no friends to hang around with, no place to go since I couldn't cross my boundary lines, and parents who couldn't find any time for me. They just argued and fought; like the night before, so loud that I just lay in bed and cried. I was tired of it. No one cared. It was as if I didn't exist. That's why I wanted a new start; a new beginning.

"It's time," I said with determination.

I got up, disregarded the dog that sat looking at me with his head cocked, and went quietly back into the house. Going silently down the stairs, I got the bag that held my only real possessions. As my mom talked on the phone, I snuck back outside, got on my bike, and was ready to take on my new life.

II

I slowly coasted down the long cement driveway and onto the paved street. There was water in the curb-gutter from a previous rainfall, so I drove my tires through it, splashing water over myself, and watched as the tires painted their lines on the dry pavement. I then slapped myself on the behind as if whipping the reins upon a horse's rear, and started to peddle, my feet and legs going into motion. After I'd gone far enough, I screamed 'ya-hoo!' I couldn't help but smile. I took a deep breath, smelling; tasting the scent of flowers. The first few blocks were fantastic. I felt new, energetic – ready to go forever! It was just like a person who could suddenly fly. I held my bag in one hand and drove the bike with the other. It finally felt as if I was on my own. A new person. I had visions of where I was going. Some place great. It would be miles and miles away, among pine trees, birds, and other animals. I'd find new friends, live on my own, build a fort out of logs. No more listening to fights; no more crying at night.

I noticed my shadow as it followed closely behind. "Howdy, Straw, I mean, Nick Findley; you naughty boy!" I laughed. I continued peddling for several blocks, driving beneath the shade from the trees that grew along the street, smiling the entire way. Smiling, that is, until my eyes suddenly detected the dark-enameled words.

Instantly my feet stopped and reversed their motion. My rear tire skidded rubber on the payment as I felt my insides sinking.

It was the boundary line. The imaginary boundary my parents had told me never to cross by myself. It limited my wanderings so they would always know my general location – Thomas Street. My bike stopped just before the street sign, its words looming above me. Cars began to swish by on the three-lane highway that led to the center of town. "Good thing," I said. "Can't cross till all those cars pass."

I drove in circles before the intersection. It was as if a mighty gorge lay before me and I needed a running leap to cross it. Every time my bike would point toward the other side, my stomach would go empty, and then fill with a rushing wind that swirled against my insides. Voices inside me were arguing. One saying, "Now's the time, go ahead," while the other would say, "Maybe it would be better to go tomorrow. Maybe you forgot to bring something." The longer I waited, the worse it got.

Finally, I stopped. I saw that my shadow had disappeared as I sat on the bike next to the curb.

"Do _something_", the voice said again. Yet I remained motionless, staring down the street, seeing the long line of shadows from the overhanging trees as they blurred at my vision's end. I felt weak, more alone than ever.

I never noticed the cars as they passed, not even the one which turned at the corner and stopped alongside me.

"Well, funny meeting you here," a familiar voice spoke. "What ya up to today, Straw?"

Suddenly I could feel my cheeks getting hot; my hands began to perspire. I tried to hold my bag behind me, to conceal the tip of my fishing pole as it stuck out, then slowly turned to confront the smiling old man. "Oh, …uh, hi Grandpa. I'm just out riding around. Ah – you know – nothing else to do during the summer."

The discerning sage gave a wink. "Yep, know what ya mean." He smiled broadly, then his face relaxed. "Hey, I was wondering – you think you'd like to go up north to the cabin for the weekend with your grandma and me?"

I glanced over my shoulder and took another look across the boundary…

He spoke again, "What's the matter, don't you want to?"

I quickly turned to face the sparse, gray-haired man. "Ah – yah – golly, that sure would be great. When you leaving?"

He smiled again and chuckled. "Well, if you race me back to your house and pack quickly, we'll get going today."

I had never gone to the cabin without my parents before. I quickly set my pedals in motion and shouted over my shoulder, "Okey, dokey. Last one there's a rotten egg!" I went as fast as I could. I even got angry at the bag I carried, for it kept me from going faster. I crunched it against my chest as if carrying a football, and lowered my head, focusing my eyes for the familiar green house that I had just left. My legs began to ache, but I didn't care, for I managed to beat my grandfather to the driveway and was waiting at the backdoor as he drove up.

I watched as he slowly got out of the car. His movements reminded me of Hiney, a pet turtle I used to have. I noticed his potbelly as he walked around towards me. His face had that serious look, and I had to smile.

"Ha, ha, I beat ya, Grandpa," I boasted.

"Yep, yep, but you better get packed while I go in and talk to you mother. We don't have all day, ya know."

Going quietly through the house, I went upstairs to my bedroom and began to pack, merely transferring my stuff into a duffel bag. I caught myself before I headed back down the steps. "Need to take my time or else they'll know something's not right." I sat on my bed until the heat got to me, then headed back down into the living room where my mom and grandpa were sitting.

"All set," I said with a grin.

My mother turned and looked at me with sort of a surprised and hurt look on her face.

My voice weakened. "It's alright if I go, ain't it Mom?"

She studied me with her eyes without replying.

"Please?" I begged.

"It'll be alright," she finally answered. "But *only* if you behave. You've got to do as your grandpa and grandma say. Don't think that because it's summer and you're going to be away from your mother and father that you can do as you please. Grandpa can spank you just as well as your father can." Her voice sharpened, "You hear me, Strawton?"

"Yes mom," I said in a subdued tone. "I'll be good. Honest." I lowered my head and stood silently.

Grandpa got up from his chair and started toward the door. "He'll be alright, Marie. Don't worry. He won't be a bit of trouble."

I followed behind him, reaching the door first. Just as I opened it, my mother exclaimed, "Aren't you even going to kiss me good-bye?"

'Right there in front of Grandpa?' I thought. I turned and planted a peck on her cheek, then quickly left the house and ran to the car.

As soon as Grandpa made it, we were off; first to pick Grandma up, and then on our way north to the cabin. As we drove from our house, Nick Findley passed us on his bike. He noticed me as he went by and waved; I rolled down the window and stuck my head out. "See ya later, Nick," I shouted. I saw him smile and nod in reply.

I turned and sat back, beginning to think of the cabin and how nice it'd be. Suddenly, we stopped. My heart momentarily skipped a beat, till I saw the red traffic light. Relieved, I peered from the back seat window and noticed the sign on the corner. As the light changed and we drove on, I smiled. I had finally crossed Thomas Street!

III

It took forever to drive to the other side of town, pick Grandma up, then drive back through it again. By the time we finally left the city, I was excited as a hummingbird in a flower garden. With the car door window rolled down, my left arm hanging outside, I began to have fun with the wind blowing along the car as we gained speed on the highway. I raised my hand and tried to fight the fierce current, pushing against it with my palm. It made different sounds when I turned my hand a certain way. It became an airplane, a kite, then a butterfly. I noticed someone driving a car, coming from the opposite direction. Just before we passed each other, the driver stuck his hand out the window, just like mine! He must have thought it was fun too, for he began to slowly move his palm back and forth!

After a bug smashed up against my hand, I tried to think of something else to do. Hours passed, or so it seemed, while I explored the backseat. I tried to remain as quiet as possible, for fear my grandparents would turn the car around and take me home. But some things I just had to know. "Gramma?" I asked. "How much farther?"

She glanced at Grandpa and replied, "Oh, we still got quite a ways, but it won't be long."

I watched intently as we passed more cornfields and cows. We traveled through tiny villages called Sterling and Rose City. Then I noticed that the small woodlots were growing into large ones. Finally, we turned off the pavement and onto a gravel road. I *knew* I was up-north then! We had to slow down, for there were gopher holes in the road and some large rocks. It also meant that I could start looking for animals, such as deer, among the trees and green ferns. The air was different right away too. You could smell pine trees in it and it seemed to clean your lungs out when you took a deep breath. One of the best parts of the trip was the roller-coaster ride, as we went up and down one hill after another. After a short distance, I glanced back and wondered why all the roads couldn't be like this one.

The dust stayed swirling behind the car for about half an hour more till we got to the final hill that led to the cabin. Then the road suddenly became sand, the car drove on what seemed to be a smooth lawn of grass. Coasting down, the trees began to overhang the road, leaving it as a tunnel of cool shade. It wound back and forth, a noiseless, peaceful trail, as peaceful as the entire valley where the cabin stood. As the road leveled off, the varnished logs of my grandparent's cabin could be seen through the trees. Beyond were a few other cabins, too, all snuggled amidst jack pine and scattered oak.

Just before my grandparent's place was an old wooden sign nailed to a tree next to the road. No one knew who put it there, but then nobody took it down either. It was part of the entire valley and seemed as if it just grew from the tree. On it were the weathered, red painted words:

> "Sleepy Hollow"
> City Limits

My grandparent's cabin was the best of all the others. It was a real cabin. Even had the smell of a cabin. All made of real logs, with a stone fireplace, and a bathroom that you had to go outside to get to. There wasn't any running water; I always had the job of filling a bucket from the pump outside. I remembered the one time we got there at night and my parents had to fumble around with matches to light the gas lamps – 'cause there weren't any electric lights there either! I felt just like a pioneer when I was there. Even better.

After we drove in the partially grass covered, sand driveway, I bolted out of the car like a spooked jackrabbit and began to run around in the woods looking for something to see. With an old branch of a tree that looked like a rifle, I began hunting for big game. The sun was fiery hot, but the shade of the numerous trees made it seem cool. The strong smell of the forest filled my lungs with an invigorating energy. Soon I spotted a giant buck in a clearing; I immediately fell behind a brush pile. Slowly I poked my gun out and took careful aim – but just as I was going to pull the trigger, I saw a bunch of bugs flying around my head – then I heard this buzzing sound – and next thing I knew, I was running, half screaming and hollering, back to the cabin, followed by a bunch of bees – who just happened to live in that brush pile! I was swatting all over like a madman, and you could have bet that every bee in the country was swarming me. When I finally made it back, I was crying and thought I'd die for sure, but as it turned out, I only got stung once – right on the tip of my nose! My grandma put some strong-smelling medicine on it to ease the pain, and after a few more tears, I was nearly back to normal.

I then asked her if I could use the B-B gun to shoot cans with. I sniffled and gently touched my nose with my finger, my lower lip extended as if a step for someone to walk on. After a brief discussion with instructed warnings, including the incident when Aunt Teen got shot in the eye, and that's why her eye was crooked, I was soon setting cans up on the other side of the road.

The sun was shining into my eyes as I stared across the road. While loading the BB gun, I saw some tweety birds hopping on some tree branches. I looked around; no one was watching. Carefully I took aim and let a BB go. I'll be danged if I saw a feather drop off! The bird tumbled from the branch, but just before it hit the ground, recovered and flew off. With it went the rest of the birds. "Dang," I said. "Guess I should have gotten closer before I shot."

I continued my marksmanship by knocking over the cans with the BB's. I enjoyed the sound made by each one as it struck the can. Knocking them over made me feel like Davy Crockett. After several trips to reset the dented targets, I heard the voice of my recent nurse.

"Straw! Dinner time!"

"Dang it," I said to myself. "Okay, Grandma, I'll be right there," I yelled. "Dang it," I said again as I headed for the cabin. "Every time I'm having fun, something always makes it end." I turned around and saw the positioned cans. "Well, here's one for good luck." I aimed, pulled the trigger, and heard a loud 'ting' as the can fell over. Smiling, I went into the cabin, washed my hands in the wash-pan, and was the last to the table.

After they made me say Blessing, we commenced stuffing ourselves. Grandma sure could cook! She had some homemade bread and some homemade chicken-noodle soup—with real homemade noodles. I loved eating the wide noodles; you could get them to slide right down without any effort. As I was inhaling them, I looked around and discovered that she had made one mistake—she had used too many dishes!

Following dinner, I tried to quietly sneak out so I could return to shooting cans, but Grandma's eagle eyes spotted me, and with a call of my name, I was soon next to her with a towel in hand. I noticed how large she was; I barely came up to her shoulder standing on my tiptoes. Her silver-gray hair was the most distinguishable; it seemed to give off light! Her face had faint lines streaming from her cheeks, and some of her skin around the bottom of her jaw was beginning to droop. Her hands, though, were wrinkle-free and smooth—and boy, could she wash dishes with them!

As she handed me a wet plate, I saw Grandpa leave to go fishing. I stood silently and watched through the window as he drove off. Looking up, I asked, "Grandma, why can't I go with him?"

Her gentle blue eyes gazed down at me, "I guess he didn't think you wanted to. I know your grandfather enjoys fishing with his grandchildren, but… " She paused. "Did you ask him?"

I turned my eyes from her and studied the plate I was drying. Meekly I replied in the negative. "But I never thought he'd take me anyways," I protested. "I'd probably just get in his way."

She dried her hands on her apron and placed one on my shoulder. "Oh Strawton, you don't have to be afraid of that. Why don't you ask him tonight when he gets back? I'm sure he'd be happy to take you along tomorrow."

"You really think so?" I asked.

She nodded her head.

Looking up to her gray hair, I felt an inner strength in me bubbling. "Yeah," I answered. "I think I will!" I looked out the window, visualizing his car and us going fishing. "Yeah," I said again quietly to myself. "I *will*."

After we had finished the dishes, I returned to shooting cans, but soon became bored. I went in to get ready for bed, then found some comic books to page through. I sat in a big rocking chair with a dark leather padded seat. With the sound of an approaching car, I anxiously looked up and waited for it to turn into the driveway, but it never did. I turned the page of the comic book and saw a big clay man who was super-strong and somebody who could stretch their arms a long ways and these robots from outer space who were going to take over the world. When I saw car lights shining momentarily on the walls, they looked like the beams from a ray gun. I peeked through the curtain to see the deathly shafts of light suddenly become dark. I knew it! Springing toward the door, I left the battle for the Earth on the chair and ran outside in my pajamas to stand by the car as he stepped out.

"Catch anything, Grandpa?"

"Oh, just one."

"What kind? How many inches long is it? Is it big? Where is -"

"Well hold onto your britches," he said with a smile as he slowly eased to the back of the car and opened the trunk. "There she be!" he pointed.

As the trunk light filled the opening, there laid a fish on the green mesh of a landing net, its gills still trying to breathe the air. It was as big as a whale! I began asking more questions, not leaving him alone till he had told me the whole story. As he explained his evening, it felt like I was there.

I could see him quietly drifting in the boat and casting close to a group of partially submerged tree stumps. Suddenly, as if a bolt of lightning shot through the water, a monster size fish grabbed his lure and ran off with it. Then the great fight. Jumping, splashing, diving, the pole bent over in a huge arch—the fish weaving its way through the weeds and brush, then one last rush to safety beneath a big stump. But Grandpa used the great strength in his arms; the struggling large-mouth bass slowly came to the net and was lifted into the boat.

Grandma came out just as Grandpa continued, in a different, but familiar tone.

"Yep—it sure put up a good battle, but not like the one I had on the other day." He paused and chuckled aloud. "*That* one gave me the best fight I ever had, going under logs, around stumps—why, I had to get my second pole and throw out till it finally hooked into *that* lure, then I had it on *two* poles!"

My eyes got big as if I had seen a ghost, while Grandma stood staring at Grandpa. He hesitated for a second and suddenly noticed that she was standing behind him.

"Yep—now, *that* fish—it sure was something … but we better get to cleaning this one before it gets any darker."

I was still picturing him holding two poles as we began to walk to the fish-cleaning site with the use of a flashlight that Grandma had brought out for us. The cleaning table was built behind the outhouse; a wide board nailed between two trees. When he started scaling the fish, I stood watching, biting my lower lip as I held the flashlight. He continued cleaning while I kept thinking, 'if you don't ask him now, you might never go.' One side of me said, "Go ahead, it'd be neat to fish," and another side of me said, "Maybe he'll say no." All the while that fish getting cleaner and cleaner.

Finally, I just blurted out, "Grandpa?"

He quietly replied without stopping his work. "Yes Straw. What is it?"

I swallowed hard. "Well—I was wondering. Aw—do you think I could go fishing with you tomorrow, that is, if you were going? I'll try not to be in your way, and if you don't want me to fish, I could row the boat or something. But if you don't want me to go, that'd be okay, too. I wouldn't mind. I know I'm too young and might be in your way."

The scales stopped flying.

"Well, I'll tell you what," he said in that serious tone. "As soon as we get in the cabin, it's off to bed, cause if you're wanting to go, daybreak comes awful early."

My stomach became light and did flips while my heart pounded. "You mean I can go with you?"

He laughed, and in that serious tone, "Sure you can."

Later, after the fish was wrapped with wax paper and placed into the icebox, the lights were extinguished, and everyone settled down to sleep. I got up quietly from my army cot to set my clothes in order so I could get right into them the next morning. They had a tiny oil lamp lit, so I could just barely make out the images in the dark. I then walked silently to the two doors of the cabin and made sure that they were both locked.

I had a thing about nighttime. There was a bear somewhere out there prowling around, wanting to get in, especially while I was asleep. Satisfied with locked doors, I lowered myself gently upon the cot and closed my eyes. Outside, penetrating through the darkness, came the repeated musical song of a whippoorwill. Through its melodious call, I found that the night was not entirely bad. There was at least one good spirit out there!

The next thing I knew, someone was shaking me. Drowsily, I raised my head and looked around. Through the dim light, I saw my grandfather, dressed and waiting. I closed my eyes and plopped my head on the soft pillow, then suddenly realized where I was. Jumping up, I moved as if I was a fireman and the fire alarm had just gone off.

After dressing, I drank a glass of milk and ate two chocolate chip cookies. Carrying a couple fishing poles, I went outside with Grandpa. Though *I* might have been having trouble waking up, the birds weren't. They were all singing away, making a racket. I zipped my jacket up as the cold, dew-laden air began to soak into me. I gave out a shiver and got into the car.

Meanwhile, my Grandpa hadn't said a word. He just loaded the car and kept looking through the trees and sighing like someone who had worked all day and finally got to rest.

Eventually, he got in and started the car.

"Think it's a good day?" I asked.

"Well—seems good now, but it can always change. We'll have to wait and see."

We drove down the old sandy road, the headlights barely making out the large rocks that were half-buried. After several curves and small hills, we finally started climbing upward. Reaching the top, I could see below us a large empty spot in the woods. When we drove down to it, a dense fog bank was slowly moving across what seemed to be gray-colored dirt. As I looked again, the dirt became water! We drove along the shoreline, eventually finding a place to pull off and park.

As we got out of the car, I saw Grandpa looking across the lake and mumbling something. I didn't ask him what he said. It was just a lake to me with a lot of fish. All I called it was "Bass Lake".

His small aluminum pram was waiting near the water, chained to a tree. It was easy to unchain it, flip it over, and load our gear. Soon we were sitting on the cushions and free from the shore.

I could hardly wait to get my line wet. As he rowed out among some stumps, I started casting. The water was like a sheet of glass, and as my lure hit it, the cracks undulated from it in a circle, finally reaching the boat. I kept casting till I noticed that I was casting two to three times more than my Grandpa. I smiled to myself, thinking that right then and there he wasn't going to catch as many as I, for I was covering more area and was bound to get more chances at catching a fish. I kept casting my lure and reeling it in—in rapid succession. All I had to do was to wait for one hungry enough—then I'd show Grandpa!

My bottom jaw nearly dropped to my chest as I saw Grandpa's pole bend with the first fish. I got the net out and raised the scrapper out of the water just as the morning sun was breaking through the trees and the scattered fog on shore.

"Little one," my grandpa said as he carefully worked the hook out. He stuck his thumb in its mouth and raised it by its lower jaw. It hung briefly in the sunlight before being lowered gently back into the water. "Go on and grow up," he told it as it swam away.

I sat there scratching my head beneath my baseball cap. "How come I didn't catch one? I've been fishing till my hand is tired of reeling in."

My grandfather looked at me with some kind of power running from his eyes. He pointed the tip of his fishing pole as if aiming at something, then made a half arch backward and casted. His rubber worm splashed next to a partially submerged stump and sank.

"Why don't you try fishing a little slower," he addressed me while watching his line. "Concentrate on making a good cast. Just don't throw your lure out anywhere. Place it close to the stumps—right next to them—that's where the fish are. And take your time when you retrieve your line. Tease them with your patience."

I nodded my head and paused as he began to slowly reel his line in. I wanted to prove that I was right, so I went back fishing the way that I had been. Then after a few casts, I looked at the wet net lying at the bottom of the boat and remembered the fish that was flopping in it.

On my first cast, nothing. Or my second. Then on the next one, I watched my Grandpa and did exactly what he did. Suddenly I got the biggest strike in my life. I jerked back hard—but missed setting the hook.

"That's the time when you should be fast," he said while raising his eyebrows and grinning.

Next cast I concentrated extra hard, placing the lure just inches away from where the fish had struck last. I watched as the angle of the line sank further, telling me that the lure was approaching the bottom. As I slowly began to retrieve the artificial worm, the line became taunt. I reacted by setting the hook hard. My heart pounding, my pole bent double, I pulled, but the line wouldn't budge.

"Snagged?" my Grandpa asked.

I tried jerking it free, but without luck. "Dang it," I said to myself. "Sorry Grandpa, I didn't mean to."

Grandpa set his pole down and rowed over to the hungry stump. Again, I tried yanking it free, but without success. I just knew we'd have to break the line.

"Here," he said, reaching for my pole.

I gave it to him, as I thought that my fishing days were over.

"Good cast," my grandpa said seriously. "You'll never catch fish if you don't get snagged. Your uncle Lou is the best fisherman there is and he's always snagged up on something. But he's always catching big fish, too." He reeled in some of the slack line. "When you want to get your snag free, try to reel your tip of your pole down to the lure, like this."

I watched as the end of my pole went deeply underwater.

"When it gets to the lure, take it straight down, sharply." He shoved almost the entire length of the pole into the water, then raised it with the worm dangling from its end. He handed it back to me.

I rattled my head in disbelief. "Thanks, Grandpa. Thanks a lot," I said, after witnessing a miracle. It was hard to believe that I was able to fish again. "Sorry if I messed things up".

He smiled but made no reply.

I watched as he rowed a short distance to another spot. I studied the surrounding snags that poked their ends from the water. Choosing one, I carefully casted toward it. My worm struck the gray, weathered wood, bounced off it slightly, and sank. Hardly before I reeled up the slack, I could see my line moving away from the snag! This time as I set the hook, the rod bent over in an arch, and I could feel an eluding powerful pulse in my hand. "Grandpa! Grandpa! I got one!" I yelled ecstatically.

"Keep your rod tip up," he answered. Reel him in nice and slow and easy."

The fish darted toward a stump, but I pulled back and reeled him toward the boat. The live, pulsing sensation from its swimming felt electrifying and powerful through the pole to my hand. Its energy was directly connected to me! I continued reeling, till finally grandpa did the honor of netting *my* fish.

I saw him smiling without showing any teeth. I was like a chessie cat.

"Want to keep him?" my grandfather said, while holding it out toward me.

"Naw," I answered. Let's throw him back so he can grow up."

With that, my grandfather nodded his head and lowered the fish back into the water. I watched it swim away through the clear pristine water.

Funny what one fish will do to you; boredom sure quits. I started fishing so every cast might result in the big lunker. Once more my rod bent double and I thought I had it on, but it just ended up being another submerged stump. Yep, it sure was great getting bites and catching fish, but after a couple hours, they suddenly quit—and no matter how slow and careful I fished—it was just no fun at all. I thought it'd be better to jump overboard and go swimming, especially with the hot sun baking down on us. Taking off my jacket, I saw Grandpa stretch his legs out in the boat.

"Guess we've caught all we're gonna. Think it's time to head in and get some breakfast?"

"Sure Gramps."

"Well, why not row us in and we'll be out of here," as he pointed toward shore.

My heart began to race as I carefully moved to the middle seat.

"Just take your time and look where you're going," my grandpa instructed.

After I maneuvered the boat to some open water, I dug the oars in and watched the bubbles and the water turn white behind the boat. My stomach was growling bad, so it didn't take long before we touched land. I had made the entire trip without even running into a stump! Quickly, I helped load everything into the car and chained the boat to a tree. Before we left, I pulled the fish-stringer out of the lake and admired the five bass we had caught. Two were mine. Proudly, I lowered them on newspapers in the trunk and got in the car.

As my Grandpa drove slowly back to the cabin, I looked at the old fisherman. We hadn't said many words down at the lake, yet it seemed that I knew him better than I ever did before. He sure meant a lot to me—and so did those fish he helped me catch—especially after we got back, and he took my picture while I was holding them in front of me. And to top it off, I even got to clean them!

While scaling them, no other fish got so much attention. I wanted them to be fit for a King. When I figured they were done just right, I rinsed them off at the pump and took them in where they were placed into the icebox, wrapped in wax paper. Breakfast was ready, so I sat down to the table and began talking, telling Grandma about the fish we had caught.

After Grandpa was done eating his huckleberry pancakes, he got up from the table and went outside. I quickly finished and followed him out. He was heading for the forest across the road, so I asked if I could go along. He nodded and said the magic word.

At first, while he walked on the old logging trail, I ran through the heavy ferns among the pine trees trying to catch a glimpse of a deer, squirrel, or some animal. After trampling through the brush and undergrowth and seeing nothing, I finally came back and walked with him.

He walked slow—so slow that my bones began to itch for movement. He was quiet too; his feet missed every twig on the path.

"Oh hang, Grandpa," I whispered. "We ain't going to see anything. I know we ain't. I just took a quick look-see and there's nothing out here, except trees."

He didn't say a word, just continued to walk. Once in a while he'd stop, his head would turn slowly in a semi-circle, like a periscope out of water. As we went farther down the trail, I noticed that I was walking nearly step for step with him. I even tried to be more noiseless than him. Suddenly he stopped and pointed with his arm. My eyes followed its direction and there stood two deer looking right at us! I took a step to get closer to them, but they jumped and ran off, sticking their white tails straight up in the air like a skunk ready to release its frustrations.

"Neat Grandpa, neat!"

He nodded and whispered, "Yep, good-looking deer."

Before our walk was over, my guide had pointed out a couple scampering black squirrels, a lazy porcupine in a tree, a partridge (which he flushed), a bunch of woodpeckers, jays, and other birds, and a lot of deer tracks. What amazed me was, we saw them right from the trail; we didn't have to go stamping through the woods—and when we took our time and moved slowly and quietly—we saw more animals!

As we were leaving the small trail, I looked at him and asked pleadingly, "How can I get close to those animals? They always seem to take-off before I get near them."

He looked downward and closed his mouth so that his thin lips became thinner. Then he spoke quietly, "They got to trust you. You have to be patient and friendly with them."

"Friendly?" I said. "How could I be friendly with them?"

His face changed as before. "You gotta act special towards them. You got to become part of them."

'Part of them?' I thought. I slowed my pace and didn't say anything. The rest of the walk I remained silent, my eyes squinting as I stared into the surrounding forest, seeing only the bright green ferns and the tall Jack Pine and Oak trees.

When we got back to the cabin, I wanted to go out and try seeing animals by myself. With my grandparent's permission, I quickly made for a different part of the woods and went in—slow, and scanning the area with my eyes like radar, the way the Indians used to do.

Sometimes I'd see something move—but at second glance, it was nothing—just a branch or fern moving with the breeze. Other times I'd hear 'em; I *knew* I did. But there was always a mass of brush obstructing my view. The search continued this way for over an hour, until I started getting tired. After seeing only a few glimpses of birds, I sat down next to a tree, taking a quick rest.

"How can I get close to them?" I said disgustedly. Re-tying the laces on my tennis shoes snugly, I got up and looked around. "Where are you?" I shouted. "Come on out!" My eyes took a last glance through the bright green ferns and oak leaves. Starting off, I left the barren forest.

That evening while I was helping with dishes, I saw Grandpa sit in the old, high-back rocking chair. As he opened an issue of Outdoor Life to read, I wandered over to him while wiping a big pan. "Grandpa?" I asked. "How come I didn't see anything when I went out by myself this afternoon?"

He set the magazine down while rocking in the chair, the wrinkles in his face becoming more distinct.

"You can't see 'em all the time. Just like when we were fishing, we couldn't catch fish all morning. Animals are more apt to come out only during certain periods of the day; and they won't come to you when *you* want to see 'em—you got to go to *them*—and maybe they might not want to see you anyways. They're just like people; you can't all the time be friends with someone that you want to be friends with—cause maybe they just don't want to be friends with you." His eyes never left me as he continued, "You have to be patient and study 'em carefully from a distance and get to know what they do and what they enjoy. The more you know about 'em, the more you'll see 'em—and maybe they'll even want to know about you."

My mouth wide open, I stood as if in a trance. Recovering, I asked, "Well, how do you know if you're friends?"

He smiled and chuckled. "You'll know," he said decisively.

That night I took what he said with me to bed, and it kept me up thinking—and I tried to forget so that I could get some sleep—but the harder I tried to forget, the more awake I got. Then finally I got to thinking about those fish that I'd caught, I had one on my line and it was taking my bait farther and farther away and …the next thing I knew, I awoke and it was morning.

It was our last day at the cabin, cause my grandpa had to go back to work, fighting fires at the "Hose House". Quietly I got up, dressed, grabbed some cookies to eat for later, then carefully unlocking the front door, snuck outside, leaving my grandparents asleep.

The birds were chirping all together, the dew was glittering and sparkling on the ground, and the air was as crisp and fragrant as a pine-smelling potato chip. I began on the trail that my grandfather and I had walked on earlier, but soon left it after getting far enough from the main road. Slowly I went through the woods, stopping and looking carefully—but seeing nothing. In the distance, I could hear more birds singing. My eyes soon began to feel like a waterlogged sponge. It was as if the very first time I had really used them. Overhead, the deep blue sky had an occasional fluffy silver-gray cloud; the sun was yet concealed by the trees.

I scanned the tall oak trees for squirrels, the jungle of ferns and brush for deer. I looked for tracks, droppings—any sign or clue of life that was hidden in this new world. But as I continued, I began to notice that even the birds were becoming somewhat silent. The farther I meandered, the quieter it became. Finally, they quit singing altogether. The forest became numb; the trees stood motionless, towering above me, paralyzed. I was left with an eerie feeling—that of being the only living creature. It seemed I was an unwanted intruder, unacceptable by the forest. I continued walking, as if entering a silent chamber.

I snapped a small twig off a tree. If I couldn't *see* anything, why couldn't I at least *hear* them? Without bothering to carefully study the surroundings anymore, I shuffled my way further into the maze of trees and occasional windfall.

"Dang. Nothing—nobody. It doesn't matter. Ain't going to see anything. Just waste time. Patient and friendly, bah! All they do is hide from me." I stopped, remembering that I was traveling through an unfamiliar part of the woods. "Hang. That figures." I looked around. "I've really done it now." A tall scotch pine stood nearby, so I walked with a lowered head over to it and sat down.

"Should I start shouting for somebody to come rescue me? I've walked farther than I should have. I should have never gone so far. I should have stayed in bed." A tear swelled-up, but I blinked it away.

The sun was shining brightly, but the branches still shielded the rays, leaving a darkened shade beneath. My pant-legs were soaked with the dew from the ferns that I had walked through. There was a spot on the forest's floor next to the tree where the sun had penetrated, so I stretched my legs into its warmth. It didn't take long, and I began to see the steam evaporate from them, as if smoke from a fire.

As I started to calculate where the road lay, a chirp sent my eyes up into the pine tree. There, dancing on the branches, peeped a small bird, a curious chickadee. Astonished, I sat and watched as the little creature drew closer to me. While singing, it looked at me—it resembled the one that I had shot with the BB gun. For a moment, I felt that it was.

It continued peeping its music and watching me. The tiny bird hopped around—sometimes getting rather close—then flew off. As it flew, I detected movement on the ground. It was a red squirrel! It came up to a nearby tree and ran up and out onto a branch. It sat there pawing a pinecone in its hands and gnawing on it, the debris falling to the ground. I silently rose from my seat of pine needles and began to walk slowly over to the animal. As I did, it ran further up the tree and began chattering at me. I stopped and thought of going away but decided to approach a few feet farther and sit down.

The squirrel was excited—chattering, running up and down the tree, swishing its tail back and forth—acting like a fly caught in a spider web. It must've burned up its energy though, for it finally settled down and began chewing at its breakfast once more.

At the same time, my stomach made out a large growl. Reaching into my pocket, I took out the chocolate-chip cookies. As I began eating, I noticed that the squirrel was watching me. Suddenly it came slowly down the tree, its nose twitching at the cool air. I paused for a second, broke off a little piece, and threw it to the base of the tree. My heart pounding, the squirrel came cautiously down to it, bit into the tiny morsel, and carried it back up to its branch. I watched as his teeth tore into the tiny chunk. When it finished, it slowly came back down the tree. As it did, a winged, flighty feeling inside me started, as if a group of butterflies were all emerging at once from the same hidden refuge. When the tiny animal reached the bottom of the tree, I decided to hold out a bigger piece in my hand instead of throwing it to the furry glutton as before.

It didn't know what to do. It looked at the tree, then at the cookie, then at the tree. It inched ahead, its legs ready to spring away. I remained frozen till it finally came to my outstretched palm. Its nose twitching, his mouth opened and gently took the piece of cookie—it was so close! But instead of running, it backed off a couple feet and sat there, pawing and chewing the piece, then another that I immediately offered, and another—till there was no more! Then it quickly sprinted back to the tree branch and sat staring at me.

My heart was thumping loudly as I watched it. There was a tingling sensation running through me. I felt as if I could laugh for joy, or cry. When I arose and looked about, it was as if I could reach out and touch everything. I took another glance at the squirrel so as to be left with a memory of its smooth, reddish-brown fur and pure white underbelly.

"I'll see you again sometime. Goodbye my friend," I shouted.

As if to return a farewell, it chattered to me.

I hadn't a watch to tell the time, but I knew my grandparents would be wanting to leave, so I began walking. Seeing the sun, I visualized where the cabin lay. My eyes studied the area and detected the top of a large tree that towered above all the others; I started off toward it.

My eyes continued to be busy; I saw more birds, a few chipmunks, and I even jumped a big snowshoe rabbit! I thought of following the tan colored animal, but it was in such a hurry, I couldn't keep up! Turning from it, I approached the big tree. There ahead, lay the trail that led to the cabin. I wasn't far away from it at all!

"Grandpa was right," I said while walking down the narrow road. "Guess I just shouldn't rush and—well golly—I never thought it would happen. Me and that squirrel, so close that I could have scratched it between its ears—and those other animals. Gee whiz."

When I got back to the cabin, I was somewhat hesitant to go in—for I had snuck out that morning without permission. Just to be safe, I had a plan ready. I would simply tell them that I'd lost my compass the day before and was out looking for it. The truth was, I had never owned a compass, but they didn't know that.

As I opened the door, my anticipated frowns and lecture were absent; instead, I was greeted with their smiles. My look of seriousness vanished; I quickly began telling them of the animals I had seen.

Grandma's face brightened up right away when I mentioned the rabbit. And Grandpa, well he had that strange smile, the one without showing any teeth, as if it were coming from somewhere else. And he had that look in his eye—it made me feel nearly a foot taller!

Following a hasty breakfast, I started to pack for the trip home. I couldn't believe how the weekend had gone by, lickety-split. It seemed that we had just unpacked the car, but now we were packing it again! Soon we were backing out of the driveway and traveling through the tunnel of overhanging trees and up the steep hill. As the car jerked into low gear, I sat quietly, thinking about all that had happened. The fish, the forest, the animals.

They were quiet, while I was thinking. The car was slowing as it approached the top of the hill. Everything would go too fast when we started back down, so I knew I had to talk now.

"Grandpa and Grandma?" I said as I leaned toward the front seat. "Do you think it'd be all right if I came up to the cabin next time with you? I sure like it up here."

I knew from their smiles before they even spoke. "Of course you can, Straw," answered Grandma.

"You betcha," Grandpa echoed.

I smiled a broad smile. Sitting back, I stared out the window, as if viewing the ferns, brush, and trees. Instead, my eyes were seeing the big fish that lay on the bottom of the boat, entwined in the bright green landing net, its huge gills slowly moving back and forth—the tiny chickadee hopping branch to branch, upside down at times, cocking its head back and forth, peeping—its beady black eyes looking at me—and the red squirrel sitting before me, its teeth crunching into the crisp cookie, tiny crumbs falling onto the brown leaves and pine needles. I was petting it as it sat next to me—scratching it between its ears —

In the distance, I heard a gentle voice. I opened my eyes as the car suddenly stopped; my Grandma was turned around toward the back seat, smiling at me. I glanced out the window, noticing the familiar, green-painted house. For a moment, I forgot that I had left it; the weekend seemed only a dream, as if my wishes had come true only during my sleep. But seeing my duffle bag, my thoughts whirled to the log cabin of my grandparents. I hesitated as a collage of scenes whisked through my head. Sighing, I finally opened the car door and got out.

After a brief exchange of thank yous and a re-emphasized promise of a return trip, I stood back from the curb and waved to my grandparents as they drove off. I was smiling bigger than ever until I turned and started toward the house. Seeing it, I suddenly felt heavy inside. Instead of going in, I decided to sit on the steps of the front porch.

"Home. Dang it." I said to myself as I rested my chin on my hands. "Now it's back to *this*. I hate it. Hate it!" I stared at the cracks in the sidewalk. Slowly a smile spread across my face. I looked at my duffle bag, visualizing the paper grocery bag. "Tomorrow morning," I whispered. "Tomorrow."

I glanced up. Someone was shouting, calling my name. I turned my head and saw a boy crossing the street, carrying something in his arms. It was Nick Findlay.

"Hey Straw, how ya been? I've been looking all over for you. Wanted to show you something. See?" He held out a tiny dog as he approached the steps.

"Hey!" I reached over. "That's my beagle!" The dog yipped as I grasped it and pulled it from Nick's hands. As it cried out, I caught a glimpse of the boy's face. His eyes were big, already beginning to fill with tears. His empty hands were still extended; the pup was looking back at him, hanging limply. But it was that painful look on Nick's face.

I laid the pup in his hands. Nick looked up at me puzzled. "Gee. I-I- I thought it was mine, but it ain't. This one's different. It's a little bigger than the one I had." I began to scratch the dog's head. The beagle's tail began wagging as Nick hugged it. "It's a neat dog, Nick. Really neat."

The boy was petting it. "Ya think so?" he asked.

"Oh, for sure. It's terrific; so friendly and…" I glanced up at Nick, "I can tell it really likes you."

"Really?"

"You bet," I replied.

He was hugging the dog closer, smiling.

"What ya been up to, Nick? Having a good summer?"

"It's been great. Especially with this." He nodded his head toward the pup. "How about you?"

We laughed as the beagle began licking his face.

That night as I crawled into bed, my mother came into the bedroom and turned on the light.

"That's my boy. I'll help tuck you in."

I lay on my back as she folded the clean smelling sheet and light blanket under my chin.

"Sounds as if you enjoyed your weekend with Grandpa and Grandma. At least by the way you talked at dinner tonight."

I smiled. "I sure did. It was just so—oh, just really neat! I'd sure like to go again."

She sat on the edge of the bed. "I'm glad you had a good time," she said tenderly. "I imagine you'll get to go again before too long, but we'll have to wait and see."

"Gee." I propped myself up on the pillow. "That would really be …" I paused. "But I can't go right away."

She frowned. "Oh? Why not?"

"Cause. I'm going to start helping Nick train his new beagle tomorrow. We had a good talk this afternoon and decided that the three of us could teach it stuff."

"Three of us?"

"Yah. Mark too."

"I see." She began to mess with the hair on my forehead, her gentle fingers caressing as if a comb. "Oh, by the way, thanks for cleaning the basement tonight. Your father and I sure appreciate it."

"Oh, that's okay. I just thought I'd do something since you let me go up-north."

She smiled again as her eyes glistened. She bent down and kissed me on the forehead. "Good-night, Strawton."

I watched her as she walked away. She switched the light off and left to go downstairs.

"Good-night Mom."

I could see her glance back in the dark. "Sweet dreams."

As I heard her quietly walk down the stairway, I leaned out of my bed and glanced out my opened window. There above the streetlight, a bright star shined.

It was huge! Lying back, I nestled into the bed. "Who knows?" I said with a smile. "Twinkle, twinkle little star, how I wonder what you are. High above the world so bright, I wish I may, I wish I might, have the wish I wish tonight!"

I closed my eyes and took a deep breath till my lungs were completely full. Exhaling slowly, I saw the puppy dog, the tweety bird, the squirrel. There were deer, a rabbit, and a porcupine. They were all gathered together. In the silence, I heard what they were listening to. Crickets! There were crickets chirping nearby. My ears strained to hear them. It was as if they were singing! I hadn't ever noticed them like that before. I listened while their sound seemed to fade farther and farther away—till I was in a deep and peaceful sleep.

THE END

ple
"A Boy's Death"

It was Sunday.

Jim snuggled down into his new red-plaid Mackinaw as the cold November morning air seeped through, causing him to shiver spasmodically. The fourteen-year-old boy thought of the cabin and the warm, genial bed, which he had left less than an hour before. As he shivered again, he wished that he could be curled into the nest made of heavy quilts and sleeping.

It was the first time the boy had sat in this old, crumbled-log blind, surrounded by its dank, musty, rotten wood smell. He wished the warm sun would quickly rise and bring with it the illuminating light. He carefully pulled out of his pocket five lead-tipped copper bullets, and lowering the lever action, opened the chamber of the 30-30 Winchester. He held one of the brass in front of his face and softly kissed the bullet. "This one's for you," he said quietly, visualizing his Grandpa. With the aid of a flashlight, he dropped it into the chamber, racked the lever closed, and gently lowered the hammer onto the firing pin. He carefully slid the other four into the magazine.

He crunched up the large black plastic garbage bag that had covered the log he was sitting on, and stuffed it behind his back, between him and the oak tree he leaned against. Feeling the cold again as the rifle lay across his thighs, he thought of the evening before, the warmth from the Franklin Stove, the fire of jack pine hissing and popping, the dim light flickering with the flames as he lay in the dark room on the couch beneath the heavy, handmade quilts.

It had been a short night; hardly a night at all, thanks to the men talking around the kitchen table. For the most part, they had ignored him, except for the brief command shouted from his Uncle Richard to "make sure you slit your deer's throat tomorrow, Jimmy. And stay in that blind and don't go walking around, or you'll get shot just like Les did. Even wearing red won't save ya."

That was it. They talked as he stood in the half-darkness on the linoleum covered cement floor of the living room, folding his clothes and placing them on the seat of the straight-back wooden chair next to the couch. His pajamas were left in his duffel bag; he figured he'd save time if he was already in his new thermal, long-john underwear when he woke. Only when everything was ready for the next day did he crawl beneath the heavy quilts and lay his head on his folded sweatshirt. The wavering light from the Franklin stove dimly brought to view the objects of the large living room of the varnished log cabin. Behind him were the half-walls of the two bedrooms for the grown-ups. On each of the walls was a huge wall-paper picture; one of a giant buck with two does standing among some maple trees, their branches displaying brightly colored orange, red, and yellow leaves, the ground ablaze with the same, while the other picture had two massive bucks jumping over a snow-covered blow-down. There was the living room with a huge brown rocking chair, and a smaller black one, and the couch. In one corner was the woodstove, the other corner, an oil heater. The kitchen area, which had once been a screened-in porch, had a large rectangular shaped table, which the men sat around.

Where he lay, the wooden chair partially blocked the light coming from the kitchen. Since he wasn't sleepy, he reached over and took the sheathed hunting knife that lay on top of the pile of folded clothes. A gift from his grandfather. He glanced up to the round log beam above the center of the room. His great-grandfather's sword was displayed on the varnished log. It was the sword he used as captain in the queen's cavalry for the Belgium army before he came to America. He pulled the knife from the sheath and noticed the shiny steel reflecting in the bright light from the broad entranceway of the kitchen. As he returned the knife to its place, he could hear the men's voices from behind the kitchen wall, loud and clear.

"Oh, the hell with them!" came the angry voice from his Uncle Richard. "They show their god damn faces around me and I might just mistake them as a four-legged critter. And then, you'll read about *that* in the paper."

He could hear a glass being filled and a bottle being set down hard on the table. In the next moment, his Uncle Richard came into view as he crossed to the sink and topped his drink off with water.

His uncle Mann's voice bellowed loudly, not the calm, relaxed way he knew it. "Who do they think they are, anyways? They're so blasted high and mighty to say that hunting animals is wrong? Like they never had a hamburger before? Or I imagine they've never eaten chicken or fish or any other animal as far as that goes?" He paused to take a swallow from his glass. "Hell, if they want to put a stop to all killing, then the next time a mosquito or a tick bites you, let them bite ya' till they kill ya', 'cause we dare not kill them. And they might as well stop trying to find a cure for cancer, or any other disease. All them bacteria and viruses have a right to live, too. And Geesus, instead of all that research, look at all the money they'd save."

Frank Tavner was the oldest—and smallest—among them, just a few years older than Grandpa Jim. His wrinkled brow moved up to his thinning, gray hair. He stared out the window, into the night, a smirk on his face, while pouring a little more Beam into his glass.

"Now boys," he said wryly. "You're just a bunch of savage, meat eaters, shootin' every poor little critter in sight. It's about time you put away your guns and start eating like rabbits."

Grandpa Jim stood at the table's end, leaning on his outstretched arms with his hands planted firmly on the plastic tablecloth. "Damn. You're right, Frank," he replied seriously. "I _love_ rabbit."

There was loud laughter.

Frank was silent for a moment. It was too early to go back to his cabin yet. He changed the tone of his voice. "Ya but times have changed. You don't need to hunt for food anymore. We've got grocery stores and plenty of food."

Richard shook his head. "You're the one with the full refrigerator and freezer. With all my bills and kids to take care of, _I_ can't afford to just keep buying food. Hell, these guys out spookin' the animals from us probably have investments in all the food stores around here and are getting fat on profits they get by jackin' the prices up." He looked over at Frank. "Crise, have you seen the price of meat? And then all those additives they put into it, the shots they give to cows, the chemicals in the feed, the preservatives. Damn."

Frank stared at his glass without answering, his lips pressed tight together.

"Oh, the hell with them," roared Richard. "They're either damn college know-it-alls, or rich, been-given-everything snobs."

"By the pictures of them, I'd say they're a bunch of hippies," added uncle Mann.

There was a brief silence as more drinks were poured and the bottle finally came to rest on the folded newspaper on the table.

Grandpa Jim reflected, his voice barely audible, his eyes focused momentarily on the ceiling, then toward his glass on the table. "All I know is, I began hunting when I was a boy. And my dad did, and his dad before him. It got us outdoors, and among the animals that were yet wild. If they say hunting is barbaric and not civilized, I say it isn't; we were born hunters. If they want to change us into another type of animal, then the hell with them. Instead of outlawing hunting, they should promote it in order to bring us back in touch with the world the way it was, the way it *is*, that we still are part of. We hunted for the food. And … " he paused to take a drink and glance around the table, "something more……..besides, those animals know it when they're being hunted. It becomes a way to outsmart them." He paused again, this time to release a deep belch. "Contrary to what I read about these non-hunters, we never enjoy seeing an animal die. We do it as quickly as possible, and to take care of the meat so it isn't wasted. Hunting is a time to prepare, to go by myself or with others." He looked over at Frank who immediately responded by raising his glass to the center of the table.

Glasses began touching and the contents quickly dispensed. They were re-filled again. More words continued, then the words became songs, songs of the Mills Brothers.

The fire popped and released a bright flare of light into the room as the boy stared across to the deer head mounted on the wall, its large antlers reflecting the light. It was nearly a perfect symmetrical rack, the dark, heavy tines, six on each side, becoming nearly white, like ivory, at the tips. The boy closed his eyes and imagined such a buck walking through the brush as he held his rifle up, taking aim at the moving animal.

The cold morning air caused Jim to shiver once again. He took hold of the rifle that was lying across his thighs. The old gun's brown stock and forearm were faded and scratched from use. The smooth steel barrel, though, was polished as if new, and blacker than the darkest storm cloud. It had originally been his grandfather's first deer rifle, then it was his dad's first, and now it was his.

He had practiced shooting the great gun during the past summer at a local gun range near his home. Under his dad's guidance, he could hit the target with every shot. He enjoyed the sound of the gun, as well as its recoil. Being able to absorb the gun's kick without moving backwards was a sign of being a man, he thought. It was as if someone was punching you. The boy took pleasure in winning over the gun's punch.

While practicing, he would smile when the bullet would smash into the sand embankment, causing the dirt to jump into the air as if a small bomb had exploded. He would often dig the mushroomed fragments of lead out of the ground and keep them to show to his school friends.

Jim gently rubbed his fingers along the cold barrel. 'Will I be able to shoot it this morning?' he thought. 'And if so, what kind of shot will it be?'

He stared into the darkness. He seemed to know everything needed to be a deer hunter. He'd taken tough shots, impossible shots, even easy shots, all rehearsed over and over again within his mind. He had imagined everything that could possibly happen.

He stuffed his glove-covered hands into his coat pockets to warm them. It was summer and his family was in the car traveling. They would often travel the dusty back roads through the pine forests in the evening looking for deer. He had the "deer eyes," especially the time when he had pointed out a deer standing behind some brush. They had stopped and everyone looked but couldn't see it. No one would believe him; but he knew it was there, even though at times he couldn't see it either. He knew it was. He just knew it.

And then another time when he had left the cabin in the morning and went out to stalk deer. He grinned as he re-pictured the big deer he had crept within a few feet of. Then another strange idea arose. Could he have killed that deer after seeing it so close? 'Sure,' came his first response. But then he remembered that it was just like a pet dog or horse; he could almost reach out and touch it — and he would have liked to.

But his grandfather had killed one, his dad as well, and to him, it seemed that it was just a steady, skillful aim and a pull of a trigger. The gun would do the rest.

But was it right to kill? In Sunday school, they taught, "Thou shall not kill." But that was for killing humans, wasn't it?

Jim opened the chamber of the 30-30 and with the aid of his flashlight, checked to make sure that a cartridge was in place. Seeing the golden head and bronze round primer of the shell, he closed the chamber of the lever-action and gently lowered the hammer onto the firing pin.

Suddenly a shot rang out; it seemed to be very close. It was still pitch black out; he couldn't see a thing. Then came a volley of shots, and another from far away. One shot after another, like a war, a barrage. Jim gripped the rifle tight and strained to see through the darkness. He couldn't see a thing.

"There must be deer all over the place", he said to himself.

The darkness remained long after the first shots were fired. Jim grew tired of staring into it, his eyes became heavy, and he finally nodded off while leaning against the large, burr oak tree.

Another loud rifle-shot rang in his ears. Jim jerked his head up. For a brief moment he thought he had slept through the day and now it was the twilight of evening. In that instant, he felt remorse, ashamed that he had failed and wasted the entire day. But then the sound of a raven calling made him realize that it wasn't true; it was yet morning. His spirits suddenly changed. He took a deep breath and knew that it was still his first day of hunting.

He turned his head and was able to make out the forms of trees and brush. He was slightly above everything, on top of a small knoll, encompassed by a few small Scotch pine and large oak trees. In front of him was a dense mass of young poplars. Behind him, in the distance, was a ridge of tall maple trees and more oak. He knew the deer had a runway from the poplars to the oak trees.

Jim heard something running on the ground and quickly jerked his head to see a lone fox squirrel scamper across the floor of golden-brown leaves. It climbed high in an oak tree and sat watching on a limb while chewing on a tiny acorn. Jim smiled.

The trees were bare, except for a few oak that held diligently to their leaves as if to resist the coming of winter. Jim could see a long way through the trees.

As his eyes scrutinized the terrain, the sound of a twig snapping suddenly pierced the forest air. Jim fought the urge to move as he stared toward the thick poplar growth. His heart began pounding hard and his breath became deeper and more frequent. Something started kicking in his stomach. His right thumb slipped to the hammer of the rifle.

He could detect movement now – coming from the thick poplar growth. He gradually raised the gun to his shoulder and cocked back the hammer. He peered down the oiled black barrel and placed the beaded sight upon the movement.

It slowly came through the stand of trees, angling off to Jim's right. Jim's index finger moved over the trigger guard anxiously. He couldn't tell what it was. It was just movement and it never stopped or slowed its steady pace. Now he could hear distinctly leaves crunching, twigs breaking. He picked out an opening just ahead of it. He'd shoot when it came into view.

Jim lowered the cold barrel of the Winchester. It was a man! Someone was walking on the deer runway. Jim expelled a deep breath. He watched as the person continued to walk through, without stopping or glancing around. He could hear a bell. Jim sat back. "Crap," he said to himself. "There goes my hunting…" He lowered the hammer and closed his eyes. 'Good time to rest', he thought. Nothing coming around here for a while.

Even though the gunshots were not as frequent, they continued, periodically. He never thought there'd be so many hunters. He wondered again, "What the hell was that guy doing? He almost got killed". He shook his head, "Damn idiot".

He leaned up against the tree again, relaxing his head and allowing his eyes to slowly blink, almost shutting them completely.

He kept seeing the movement through the poplars. The bead of his rifle and the movement, then that guy walking in that same red-plaid jacket as his own. His finger nearly touching the trigger.

The daylight grew stronger.

He kept looking for a deer. Behind him, at each side, in front of him. He kept turning his head, seeing the same things, trees and brush and more trees. Then it came to him, 'stop moving, let them come, but don't scare them away with your movements.' He stopped, leaned his head against the tree as if frozen, and waited.

And waited. At times his eyes would close, and then he'd blink them open again.

Far off, he thought he heard more leaves crunching. 'Another hunter?' he thought. The noise was coming from the same direction as the other, earlier intruder. Once again he couldn't see anything, just hear the leaves crunching. 'Damn squirrels', he said to himself. But as he strained to hear the noise, something told him that it was louder than that made by squirrels. His heart again began to pound loudly in his chest as he raised his 30-30 and cocked the solid steel hammer back. There was no mistake this time. It had to be a deer. He strained to see the animal as it slowly made its way out of the poplars.

The deer stopped, hesitated, giving a glance over its shoulder. It stared in the poplar growth, then turning with lowered head, resumed its wary walk. Soon it was out of sight, vanishing into the forest's protective maze of trees and undergrowth, without noticing the impatient black barrel that had followed it. Jim took a couple deep breaths. His heart was still beating loudly.

"Coulda blasted her," he whispered to himself.

Jim was about to lower the cocked hammer into its original position when another glimpse of movement caught his eye. Something else was moving through the poplars, following the same route in which the doe had traveled.

The boy was again ready. The pointed barrel, shaking more than usual, centered itself on a moving brown patch. The animal stopped once before coming out of the stand of thick poplars. As it left the security of the dense cover, it stopped again, broadside to the moving bead of the 30-30 Winchester's sight.

It was a spikehorn. Something was wrong with one antler; it was partially broken off. The other antler was long, straight, and pointed. They looked like the horns of a devil. As the deer paused, Jim noticed its smooth, brown coat. The deer lifted its right front leg and stamped the ground with its hoof. He then stood motionless; it's tail straight up.

The buck looked much bigger than the boy had expected.

Jim's index finger entered the circle of the trigger guard. He tried to steady the weaving barrel, but could not. He took a deep breath. For a brief moment, his eyes closed. When he opened them again, he met the stare of the deer's eyes.

Jim suddenly jerked the trigger. Without a sound, the hammer fell instantly, striking the firing pin.

Out of the cloud-black barrel came a flash, like lightning, and a roaring explosion that shook the stillness of the air, like a huge clap of thunder. As the smoke left the barrel, the lever of the rifle was working by itself, ejecting the smoking, empty casing and feeding a new shell into the chamber.

Through the gray, dense smoke, Jim saw the deer begin to run, as if untouched, leaping high and far through the entanglement of trees and undergrowth.

The young hunter's barrel followed the animal as he pulled the trigger for a second time. Again, the barrel spit out a flame and shook the air with its loud voice. But the running deer never faltered. He leaped a few more times, and except for a last glimpse of the erect white flag, was out of Jim's sight.

Jim hadn't noticed the jolting recoil of the stock upon his shoulder. Or the ringing sound in his ears. He was now out of the blind and running in the direction of the fleeing buck. It wasn't until he started up the ridge of oaks and maples and felt out of breath that he stopped, heaving in huge amounts of air through his clenched teeth. His heart felt as if it was pounding in his throat. He had to swallow in order to breathe more. A strained smile formed on his face. "I got him," he said jubilantly. "I know I did. Damn he was big. My first deer and I got him."

As his breathing slowed, he started walking, scanning ahead to see if he could detect any movement. He fed a couple more bullets into his rifle and continued searching ahead, his eyesight straining as if to bring to focus the horizon of the forest. The boy squinted so he could see farther ahead. He walked, then stopped and listened, then continued walking again. He crossed the ridge of oak and maple trees and descended down into a maze of young, thick Scotch pine. He kept looking ahead but saw nothing.

Seconds faded into minutes. Finally, it struck him. He hadn't seen the deer. He finally stopped walking.

"How could he have vanished? He had to be hit badly. He's got to be around here." Jim suddenly began to think of the wounded deer lying somewhere – bleeding. He did not want to think about it, but his mind kept picturing the restless deer hidden in some brush, dying slowly. He wished that he could locate him soon.

He stood silently. His eyes kept penetrating through the trees when they accidentally glanced to the ground. There, they remained fixed upon the fallen leaves. He nodded his head.

The boy turned and began to walk in the direction, which he thought, led back to the blind. At first, he had trouble figuring out the right way, but the ridge of tall oak and maple trees, which stood out among the rest, caught his eye. He picked out a tree and headed for it. Before long, he was back to the patch of poplars and the square pile of logs.

Once at the blind, he envisioned where the deer stood when he had fired the first shot. He walked over to the spot and began searching the ground. A smile appeared as he picked up a patch of deer hair. The whitish brown color stuck out clearly on the dark leaves. From there, he followed where the deer had run and quickly found what he was looking for --- a splotch of blood.

"Yes!" he said definitively. "Now I'll find him!"

The boy began once more, keeping his eyes to the ground and following the tiny red spots of fresh blood that had dropped upon the dry, crisp, brown leaves. The blood trail took him nearly to the same area that he had just previously wandered to.

Jim stood upon the ridge of oak and maple trees once again. He could see that the deer had crossed somewhere down below him into the new growth of Scotch pine. As he observed the fresh black dirt, left from the deer's hooves as it had sprung down the hill, he suddenly saw movement. Immediately his gun came to his shoulder. Above the end of the barrel, not ten yards away, movement appeared as a large bird. The gun barrel swung and pointed straight at it. The boy cocked the hammer back.

The ruffed grouse's head bobbed up and down like a pigeon's. It's rear tail feathers spread out like a fan, its body puffed up so it looked twice its normal size. As Jim watched the strutting bird, the bead of his gun weaved just under its head.

The boy's arms relaxed as he brought the gun down, his thumb hooking the hammer as he gently lowered it upon the firing pin. "You're dead, pat", he said to himself. He smiled as the bird began to chirp nervously. Its head suddenly lowered itself unto its breast, then it charged into a mass of dead ferns. As Jim took a step toward it, the bird exploded from the ground and made a zigzagging flight into the thicket of Scotch pine. The boy's heart responded with an instant rush of pounding. His body recoiled from the whirl of feathers taking to the air.

He shook his head and exhaled a deep breath. "Damn bird," he said aloud, once again composing himself.

Jim focused on the deer's blood trail, which had been easy to follow, but now as he approached the scotch pines, began to disappear. On top of that, he started feeling an occasional drop of rain. As he entered the pines, he lost the blood trail completely. He re-tracked, but still the blood drops ended at the beginning of the Scotch pine. He then started to scan the area in semi-circles, probing each time farther into the young Scotch pine forest, but finding nothing.

Standing in the obstructing, bushy pine trees, the boy once again thought that he had lost the deer for good. He pictured it again, just before he had pulled the trigger. It was so beautiful. It reminded him of the one he had crept up on. Then he visualized the dying deer somewhere far away. He did not want to think about it. Instead, it came to him that perhaps he had only flesh wounded the deer.

"He's not bleeding anymore. He's probably still running and not even hurt." The boy nodded his head in assurance.

"Well, he was running hard through the poplars. It was a tough shot, but I took it. It just missed him, though. I saw it strike a tree underneath him as he leaped high into the air." The young hunter started to smile. He knew that he could say something—if he had to.

But then it was no good. His mind kept showing the black barrel and the beaded sight of the 30-30, and the smoke and the deer's instant reaction to the bullet. He was somewhere in the forest, wounded, probably dying, and the boy could do nothing. He felt sorry now. He wished that he had not shot at him this morning. He wished that he had not even seen him. The more he thought, the more he wanted to be back in the cabin. He never wanted to go hunting again.

He continued walking, searching ahead for the buck. Soon the pines got even thicker and closed in on him, blocking his sight and slowing his progress. He staggered through the branches and undergrowth, until a limb snapped back at him, slapping his face and striking his eyes with the long, sharp needles. The painful sting caused them to swell with tears. He began fighting the branches, breaking those that got in his way. He was swearing and cursing loudly as he tripped over a branch of a fallen tree. Instinctively, he stuck his gun out as a crutch to slow his descent. It, too, was torn from his hand as they both crashed to the ground. Retrieving the rifle, he noticed dirt hanging from its muzzle. He felt like throwing the whole thing away, but instead, quickly found a small stick and began to poke the dirt out of the barrel. Getting up, he began to break anything that looked like a hindrance to him. Walking faster, he closed his eyes and bulled his way through the thick pine growth until he suddenly felt free of the restrictive branches. He was standing in a small clearing.

As he paused to catch his breath, he shook his head to remove the twigs and pine needles from his red hat. "It's gone," he said to himself. "You'll never find it. Damn thing. I'm just wasting my time. I can't believe it didn't drop. I must've just blown a little hair off it. Oh well."

He took a step and suddenly a deer jumped up from across the clearing. Jim jerked the gun up instantly and the deer jolted to a stop and glanced across the small distance of brown ferns and grass. Jim noticed the horns, the one spike shorter than the other, and a small splotch of blood on the fur behind the shoulder. The buck's deep brown eyes remained fixed upon Jim.

Jim continued to slowly raise the gun. Looking down the black barrel through the sights, he saw the waiting buck. His finger entered the half-circle of the trigger guard. He didn't want to, but he knew he had to.

The barrel weaved, and then steadied itself.

When he squeezed the trigger, he was crying, the tears falling off his cheeks, and onto the stock of the gun. With a mighty eruption, the lead-tipped copper bullet catapulted out of the steel barrel and struck the motionless buck.

The bullet knocked the deer over onto its back, its legs kicking into the air. Somehow, though, the buck attempted to stand up once more. Now looking toward the forest, it partially rose, but could go no further. Jim racked another shell in. The deer turned to face him. Then, lowering its head, its front legs crumbled, and without further struggle, the buck rolled over onto its side — the body quivering, the legs straightening, and finally, everything becoming still.

Jim eased the cocked-hammer down and lowered the smoking barrel of the 30-30. He studied the gun for a moment before tossing it into the wilted ferns and brown grass. Looking up, he saw the gray-cast sky and noticed rain falling. He turned to what he thought was the direction of the oak ridge. He couldn't see it, just the tops of Scotch pine. Water was slowly dripping off the tree branches. Everything was so quiet that the only thing he could hear was the hush of rain and the occasional sound of raindrops falling upon the dried, brown leaves.

Jim reached for the sheathed knife on his belt. He popped the snap off and pulled it free. He turned and walked through the wet grass to the deer but paused as he stood over it. Bending down, as the tears continued to roll off his face, the boy reached for one of the spikes in order to raise the deer's head and expose its neck. The other hand readied the blade. As he cried, he kept repeating hysterically,

"I'm sorry, ---- I'm sorry, I'm sorry, -------------------- "

The moment his hand grasped the deer's antler, Jims' eyes widened. He felt in his hand the disparate power of life suddenly awakening.

The deer's head sprung back, piercing its sharp horn into the boy's hand. Its legs kicked as it bawled to get up. One of its hoofs caught the boy's shin, sending him backwards, as he clutched his hand tight to stop the rush of blood. The boy screamed with pain as he fell to his backside. But as soon as he hit the ground, he got up. The deer's head jerked back repeatedly, its horns stabbing the air in vain. As the deer flayed its legs at him, Jim backed up and hobbled around toward the deer's backside. His heart seemed to expand in his chest, beating wildly as he crouched low and stepped to the deer's shoulder. He stretched his arm out and plunged the shiny steel knife into the deer's neck. As the deer reeled from the blade's penetration, the boy sprung back, pulling the knife out. The deer's attempt to stand intensified, its head and neck stretching upward as if to pull the entire body with it.

The boy's cry transformed into a savage cry, a cry of men in battle, of lancers on horseback charging into its foe, to kill or be killed. As the deer's head lowered, the young hunter sprung to the deer again, and with all his strength, sent the knife into the deer's neck, the blood squirting over his hands as he pulled it out and dodged the lurching horns.

The air was filled with the smell of damp humus as the deer's hoofs and horns tore into the ground. The boy's scream intensified with rage as he plunged the knife a third time, sinking it deep, feeling the vertebrae. The boy held the knife in and gave it a final thrust as he gripped the handle with both hands. His entire body shook with the deer as it quivered violently, until the deer's legs finally straightened, twitching until the last of its strength was gone.

Jim could feel the life force leave through his hands and arms. Releasing his hands from the knife, Jim fell backward onto the ground. His choked, hysteric sobs were muffled as he curled up and buried his face into the wool sleeves of his coat and wrapped his arms around his bent knees.

The steady rain was now spitting occasional flakes of snow when he heard the familiar voices of his uncle Richard and grandfather as they shouted his name. Jim stood up and wiped away the tears. The voices continued to get closer. Jim kneeled above the deer and pulled the knife out, wiping the blood on the animal's fur just as the two men broke through the pine trees and stood where the boy had stood sometime before.

"Well, I'll be!" spoke his grandpa loudly.

"Hot damn!" replied Richard, as they walked over to him. "Congratulations, Jim," as he extended his hand.

Jim's right hand gripped his uncle's tight as they shook momentarily. As he saw the other clenched, blood-caked hand, his uncles' eyebrows raised. "Hurt?" he questioned quietly.

"Naw," replied Jim as he looked down toward the deer.

His uncle smiled and bent down to inspect the deer. "You got yourself a nice size one. Hit him twice, dad. No, three times." He could see one hole through the neck, another behind the shoulder, and one at the top of the back. "Hot damn, that's good shooting. Good ole 30-30. And I see ya started to slit his throat, too. Hot damn," he repeated again.

Jim kept his eyes upon the motionless deer.

His grandpa walked up, carrying Jim's rifle. "Good job, Jim". He extended his hand.

As the young hunter grasped it, their eyes met. He noticed his grandfather smiling broadly while nodding his head in approval. It was a different kind of handshake. The grip of his grandfather's hand was firm, yet ... the boy didn't want to release it.

With his other hand, his grandfather extended the rifle to him. The boy grimaced, but only for an instant, as he opened his bloody hand and grasped the rifle. Jim tried a faint smile as he held the rifle and released his grandpa's hand.

"Yes sir," his uncle boasted, as he moved around the deer and stood in front of Jim so as to block out the boy's vision of the animal. "You're a hell of a hunter. Won't be long and you'll be out-shooting your old man and grandpa. Why you got yourself a good one. Yes sir, your first buck. You'll get some good meals from him, too."

"Yep," came the grandpa's reply. "But we better get to gutting this critter out before we get any more drenched. Besides, it's noon and I'm starving for lunch. Why don't you tell us how you got him Jim," as he put his hand on the young hunter's shoulder.

Jim stared at the eager faces of his uncle and grandpa. They were both broadly smiling.

He heard raindrops falling on the leaves. In the distance, more gunshots were fired. Jim's eyebrows rose as he took a deep breath and began to smile.

"Well," clearing his voice. "I – I," he spoke softly, looking down at the ground. "I – I saw a doe first. It was early this morning, just after some guy walked through."

"What? Some guy?" came a loud reply.

As he looked up to his uncle, his voice grew louder. "Ya, but he just walked by without stopping. Then the doe snuck through. I knew right away a buck would be nearby and sure enough out popped this here buck. He was moving fast so I took a quick shot at him and knew I had hit him and he started running and I hit him again but the stubborn thing never fell—so I tracked him to this spot."

His face resembled his grandpa's now, smiling wide, showing his bright, shiny teeth.

"I caught him in this opening just as he was running away. I had another tough shot but got a lucky aim at him and … well—" His head turned toward the motionless deer. "It was damn tough cutting his throat, though, Uncle Richard."

His uncle and grandfather laughed. "All right," approved his uncle.

Jim noticed how the forest was silent, except for the rain falling on the drum skin dry leaves, the occasional snowflake that melted as it landed, and the echoing sound of distant shots fired from somewhere deep in the woods. He momentarily glanced in the direction of the sound, but quickly turned away from it. He set his 30-30 against a tree and found his hunting knife.

As the shots faded, the smiling hunters, together, rolled the young spikehorn over and began to gut the deer out.

THE END

"Manhood"

He stood outside the Imperial Resource machine shop, the hot July afternoon sweat dripping from his Augean forehead. The walls of the building could not confine the throbbing and echoing noise of the factory. The sound of air compressors, huge boring mills, grinders, metal lathes, and the human pounding of hammer-on-steel vibrated out into the open air. It was as if the sweltering building was coughing, trying to clear its throat of the dirt and oil smoke that hung like fog above the restless machines. Outside, the strong Adonis worker turned away from the building, faced the breeze, and took a long, drawn-in breath, till his lungs stretched tight within his chest. He held it momentarily till it was no longer fresh, then released it in a tired sigh.

The sun was bright in a sky arrayed with immaculate, white clouds. The young laborer gazed across a grassy field and saw a flock of starlings flying to a couple desolate, lone pine trees. They swarmed over the trees as if attacking them, then landed till their branches were heavy laden, as if covered with black dust.

From the field, he suddenly heard a pheasant crow. The rooster's erratic, but flamboyant voice carried sharp and clear. The laborer could visualize the bird strutting—with his red and white ringed neck and colored feathers reflecting in the sunlight. As the pheasant crowed again, he thought of October, and a golden wheat-stubble with "Pat", the Weimaraner working it, the stubby tail wagging with the scent, then the abrupt point—the flurry of wings—the feel of the shotgun as it jolted into his shoulder—the explosion and sharp recoil—the bird tumbling, the feathers floating…

He laughed to himself and pictured it again. This time the bird's bat-like wings flying, gliding into another field—untouched by the spray of pellets—as he and the dog stood watching.

He smiled while a monarch butterfly flew past him, fluttering freely toward its—

"What the hell are you doing?"

The angry voice of the foreman jolted him back once again to the chaotic pulse of the factory.

"I was just getting some—"

"I don't give a damn what you were getting! You're not being paid to stand outside. Get your ass in here; you've got work to do!"

Through his young eyes, the accosted laborer briefly surveyed the middle-aged foreman whose power was in his voice. He reminded him of a choleric swine with his plump face and fat cheeks that bulged around his dark, close together beady eyes and flattened nose. As the irritated overseer cussed at him, it seemed that his thin lips never moved.

The pot-bellied man spat and returned through the door. The laborer followed, noticing a few older workers laughing quietly as he passed them. He wondered if they were laughing at his hair, or the scolding, or both. The foreman pointed with his hand toward the cement floor that was covered with metal filings and then to a push broom leaning up against a wall.

Scattering the red sweeping compound over the floor, as if scattering feed for chickens, the worker began to methodically brush the metal filings and dirt (and dried or undried splotches of spitted tobacco) into isolated piles throughout the massive building; sweeping clean till the floor's face was a whitish-gray color, listening as he swept to the sporadic voices and laughs above the rumble of the green-painted machines.

"Hey Mike, got my 440 raring to go. You should listen to that mutha scream!"

"Oh ya? Going to take it to the track?"

"Damn right. Going to enter – " Their voices fading into another boisterous pitch,

"You should have seen her. Mercy sakes, I never knew a woman could go all night!"

"No wonder your eyes are so bloodshot. Wouldn't let ya sleep, aye?" And yet another,

"Hey Gene, let's get a few of us and meet at the Stag after work."

Laughing, joking, as their machines hummed to their own conversation—while the young worker swept, imperceptible as the clean air which gently blew through the ceiling vents.

Hippo was a big man. His size alone commanded respect, but he was a kind and benevolent man, and everyone in the machine shop liked him. They say he got the name "Hippo" while playing fullback on the local high school football team. Not too fast, but watch out if you got in his way.

As he swept, the young laborer noticed him at his machine. The giant of a man looked up from his work and gave a big smile and nodded approvingly at him.

The unskilled worker returned the nod, also with a smile, and continued his job.

Near the middle of the machines, he noticed a pile of thin steel sheets on the floor. They had recently been cut by a metal saw, the edges still left with sharp pointed burrs, some resembling the tips of hunting arrows.

"Hey," he said, interrupting a tall, slender man working on a horizontal mill nearby. "That metal down there looks pretty dangerous".

The man glanced over to where the young worker was pointing. "Ya, I know. It'll get grinded down later. You just gotta watch where you're going, that's all."

The common laborer kept sweeping, carefully side-stepping around the jagged edge pile.

With much of the floor yet spewed with days of dirt and debris, the bell rang for a short break. Noticing that everyone had already left their machines and were crowded together talking and smoking cigarettes, the brooms-man began walking to the opposite end of the building where sunlight was filtering through an opened door.

The voice of Big Hippo caught the young laborer's attention. "Hey Artee, wanna get in on this week's check pool?"

Stopping, the departing worker's ears perked up with the sound of his name. It was the first time he had heard it all day. He replied in a loud voice, "Not this time—but thanks anyways, Hippo."

Nodding, the tall powerful man turned and resumed talking with the group he was standing among.

As he walked, the young laborer again noticed the gray-haired maintenance man working at his job, ignoring the bell. He admired the old man's persistence; remembering a couple days ago when he had spoken to him and he had said that he had never taken a break, except lunch, because it was too difficult to return to his job after a short interruption. As he passed him, the elder man looked up from his work.

"Well, how ya be t'day?" he said amiably.

The young laborer smiled. "Oh, not bad … and you?"

The man replied while working on the electrical light switch. "Tasame." He glanced over to the group of workers gathered at the far end of the building. "Ain't ya in on it?"

Artee turned and looked at the workers in the distance, "On what?"

"Din't ya hear?" There was a slight irascibleness in the man's voice. "Dey talking Union!"

"Union?" Artee replied.

The man looked with contempt at the group. "Da new guy, da one dey just hired. He's da one stirrin tings up. Sayin' we need to unionize... But dey ain't no reason for it," he said flatly. He returned his stare to his work. "We gettin' good pay, good ben'fits. It's good workin' here. I *know* it tis. Damn good." His voice intensified. "But dey want union, just to be union. Get paid more.—Who dey kiddin? Dem union bosses just take it!" He paused, calming himself. "Da union was good once. Long, long time ago. But now—dey ain't no good no more." He chuckled and took a brief glimpse of the other workers. "Huh, dey just cutting der'own troat. Dis here company left Da'troit because da Union kept asking fer too much. Dey not puttin' up with it here. Dey fold up --- we be lookin' somewhere else for job." He glanced at the young worker. "Why you wastin' yer time in a place like dis? You should be goin' to college. Learn to use dat' brain of yers. You got a good one, ya know." He paused and looked down at the cement floor. Slowly raising his head, he said somewhat remorsefully, "I sure wish I could have gone when I was yer age."

The young worker's face altered its appearance, not quite certain what to say. With a blink of its eyes, it returned to a look of self-assuredness.

"Ya, I'm planning to. Maybe major in something science-related, but I'm just not sure. Anyways, this job is just for the summer, to help pay for school, then I'm out of here."

"Good. Good." The elder man repeated as he nodded his head. He heard something familiar in the youth's voice. "You do just dat." He laughed to himself.

The young laborer noticed that the man was concentrating on the wires again. At the other end of the building, the group of men was still laughing, talking loudly. He started again toward the open door. "Talk to you later," he shouted.

The old man nodded, but made no reply.

Artee passed into the sunlight and sat on a concrete step. His face was distraught with his emergence from the factory. "Hell," he said to himself. "What will I do? I want to get that apartment, but...." He shook his head slowly.

The sun felt hot, the humidity unbearable. He took off his hard-hat, cooling his long, sweaty blond hair. He ran his fingers over the side of his face and lifted the curls off his ears.

Once more he noticed the swallows, diving through the air at insects and returning to the overhanging steel rafters of the roof where their nests were built. All week he had watched the young ones stretch their necks out of the nests and greet their parents with peeping, open mouths. This time as he scanned the rafters, he noticed a lone, baby swallow standing silently out of its nest, barely covered with feathers. The small bird started walking impatiently back and forth, stretching its wings out, peeping frantically.

Artee wondered if it would leap, putting into motion the rhythm of its wings, or would it just fall helplessly from the rafter?

The bell rang inside the building, suddenly ending the break period, recalling its workers back to their machines.

Artee got up, throwing his hard-hat back on, and took one last glimpse of the feathered creature upon the rafter. The bird was hesitating – standing alone, peeping as if crying, only peeping...

For the remainder of the afternoon, the young laborer worked diligently, without bothering to stop and rest. But just as he was finishing the awesome task of clearing the floor of machine waste products and their controllers' discarded litter, a chilling scream penetrated the machines' unchanging dialog.

"Crise! God damn it! Damn. Damn!!"

The pain transmitted in the voice sent Artee running. Immediately he saw a man falling backward to the floor and heard a loud 'whomp' as his head hit the cement.

A group of men had already formed a semi-circle around the fallen man. Artee separated two standing men and fell to his knees next to the injured person. He noticed the pile of jagged sharp steel and a large pool of bright red blood that was moving quickly across the floor near the man's ankle. Reaching into his pocket, he pulled out a clean, neatly folded white hankie and immediately placed it over the bloody ankle and applied pressure. He looked up directly to the eyes of Big Hippo.

"Go call 9-1-1," he shouted. Hippo shoved another man out of the way and ambled as fast as he could to the office. Artee's eyes moved to another man. "Get me some clean paper towels." His hand could feel moisture already through his hankie.

The men stood looking at each other. One finally said, "What can I do?"

"*Go get some paper towels!*" Artee yelled. "And look for a blanket".

"Blanket?" he replied dumbfounded.

Another man next to him gave him a gentle shove, "Go on, get it!"

The man shrugged his shoulders. "OK", he said quietly. He turned and trotted off to the main office.

Artee looked at the man's pale face and with his free hand, grabbed his shirt beneath his chin and gently shook him.

"Come on, stay with us, stay with us," he shouted.

He heard a moan and the man's head slowly turn toward him. He opened his eyes, blinking a few times, finally focusing on Artee. "Damn," was all he said, in a tone that Artee immediately recognized.

Hippo soon returned. Half out of breath as he shoved his way through the crowd, he said loudly, "It's on its way." Then addressing the group of men, "Boss says for you guys to get back to work."

As the grumbling faded, a man returned with a hand full of paper towels. "Here ya go," he said. "Can't find no blanket. Just this coat that's been hanging by the main door."

Artee took the towels, folded a bunch in half, and placed it over the blood-soaked hankie. "You can place the coat over his chest. And..." looking up to the man, he said in a much relieved voice, "thanks for your help".

"Sure thing." the man replied.

Hippo knelt down. "Elmer, you ok?"

Elmer's eyes opened. "Ya," he said disgustedly. "Just a little dizzy; my head hurts like hell."

"Hang in there, the ambulance is on its way."

"Damn," he replied. "I'm all right; don't need no damn ambulance." He tried rising upward, propping himself with his other hand. His eyes suddenly widened, as his eyeballs began to roll back into his head. Artee reached his arm out and caught the man's head as he fell backwards.

"Just give me a little time," he said, half unconscious.

Hippo glanced at Artee and smiled. "Sure."

The wailing of the siren, barely distinguishable at first, soon filled the entire machine shop. The neatly attired EMT's hustled in with their wheeled gurney, covered by clean white sheets.

Artee quickly relinquished his patient to the new caretakers. Wiping the blood off his hands with the remaining paper towels, he returned to his broom. As he was sweeping the last of the debris into a pile, he saw Elmer being wheeled out the main aisle, an IV bag suspended from an erect pole and tubing leading to his arm.

As the wailing of the sirens echoed throughout the shop's walls, then faded, Artee shoveled the final load of debris into a black improvised oil drum. The burdensome task was finally completed; the sprawling floor was clean, nearly as neat as if the place hadn't been used.

Artee carried his tools to the side doorway and leaned them up against the wall just as the final bell sounded throughout the building. Its last tumultuous vibrations faded quickly into a strange, deathlike silence. For a brief moment, Artee heard an internal high-pitch hum, as if listening to the Barmecidal waves from an ocean seashell. This too faded and was followed by a distant susurrant sound of men talking and of timecards being punched.

Starting toward the gathering, the blond-haired laborer passed the rows of dormant machines, leaving the clean sedate factory behind him.

As he waited in line, Artee could not stop thinking of how ridiculous it appeared—all these men standing before a gray metal box in order to insert their cards into it, as if feeding the very power which controlled the machines. Finally placing his own card into its slit-like mouth, the young laborer heard its bite and removed it to see the miraculous imprint—SAT 3:36 P.M. Trading it for his check, he saw more important digits. He smiled. Because of overtime from working a twelve-hour day, it was the most money he had ever earned. Tucking it into his shirt pocket, he began walking to the door.

Behind him, an unfamiliar voice, detached and murmured, called his name. "Artee. Artemus Herman," it beckoned.

Turning, the young laborer saw a man standing in front of the office, wearing a dark suit and tie, motioning with his hand. "Got a minute, Artee?" the man asked.

"Sure," Artee answered. It was Mr. Lokey, General Manager. He smiled to himself. He felt like answering, "Sure, Spock," the name the workers had secretly given him because of his large, pointed, Vulcan-like ears.

In the cluttered room, Artee saw the gentleman sitting at his clean desk, talking to Big Hippo. The day's earlier scene with the angry foreman flashed through Artee's mind. He readied himself.

"Artee, this will only take a second," the bossman began. "Come on in. You're acquainted with Mr. Sicyon aren't you? Hippo?"

"Yes sir," he said with a smile, while glancing at the huge man.

"Good, good." His tone of voice deepened and became business-like. "You've been here almost a month now, Artee. High School is over and, well, we'd like you to stay on once summer is over." He kept his eyes on the young laborer. "We're impressed, Artee. Not only with the way you just responded to Elmer's accident this afternoon, but by the meticulous job you do." He stopped to clear his throat, glancing briefly at Hippo. "Now whether you're aware of it or not, we offer a training program to some of our more reliable unskilled workers. It's our way of giving them a chance to learn a special trade or two and also presents them an opportunity to make more money and be able to gain other valuable benefits in the company. Hippo here says he'd be more than happy to direct you on the vertical mill, sort of an apprenticeship. It'll be some hard work, but then you'll be getting better pay once you complete the training, so—how 'bout it? Think you'd like to be a trainee here under Hippo?"

First the young laborer was silent, the unexpected puzzling him. He glanced over to Hippo, who was standing near the doorway with a big grin. Artee smiled and turned back toward the boss man.

"Gee. I never thought … but it sounds great. Sure Mr. Lokey, I'd very much be willing to try that."

The man smiled. "Excellent. That's all I wanted to hear. Report to Hippo first thing Monday, and he'll take care of you from there. And remember, if you run into any trouble, don't hesitate to see me."

"Good deal," interjected Hippo. "See you Monday, Artee." Turning, he added, "And have a good weekend, Mr. Lokey. It's a short weekend, but a weekend anyways. I'm out of here".

"Sure Hippo," came the reply. "Have a good one. See you Monday, and thanks again."

Artee hesitated while his boss took a step and reached out his hand. He glanced up and saw him smile. Reaching out, the two hands briefly grasped. Mr. Lokey's hand felt uncomfortably warm.

"Oh, and one thing more before I forget. Artee, the Company has a tradition". He reached into his pocket and pulled out a shiny coin. He raised it into the air in front of him. "Every apprentice gets a silver piece with the Company's emblem stamped on it. Just a memento; a keepsake if you want. Our way of welcoming you in." He handed it over to the young worker.

"Wow. Thanks Mr. Lokey." He examined the brilliant shine and the large initials, 'I R' on one side. The other, a bald eagle with its talon's stretched out, as if ready to strike its prey. Artee nodded his head in satisfaction and carefully placed it into his pocket. Glancing up to the eyes of his benefactor, he added, "Thanks again, Mr. Lokey".

"You're welcome," said the boss. "See you Monday, Artee".

The soon-to-be trainee walked slowly out of the peaceful, tranquil building to his waiting car. As he unlocked the door and unrolled the window of his parent's recent graduation gift, he stood staring at the swift moving cars passing by on the highway—one after another, heading north. The escaping heat billowed out of his own car as he turned and observed the factory. The last of the workers were leaving. Some were driving out of the parking lot, tires screeching onto the pavement. His hand felt the check in his pocket. A strange new power came with its touch. He glanced back to the highway of speeding cars and mumbled, "Hell, why not? Might as well join them. Time to get away, go to the cabin or …" An idea came to him. "Hey, the lake. Never did that before. Hmm, Mom and Dad will put up a fuss on such short notice, but then…."

He turned to the car and nodded his head slowly. "I'd sure like to get away."

He took a deep breath and got into his car, closing the door behind him. "Man," he said. "Just like an oven." He looked at the factory again and smiled. "Time to celebrate my new job!"

Starting his car, he sped off into the traffic, stopping only at the drive-thru bank, before reaching his parent's house.

"Artee! Artee!" screamed his sister Diana as he pulled into the driveway. She was waving her arms overhead, jumping up and down while one hand clutched something white.

He pulled up alongside her and exclaimed half-disgustedly, "What?"

"It's from Western!"

As the car engine died, Artee took the long envelope from his sister's hand and tossed it onto the seat next to him. He got out and quickly walked past her to the house.

"Aren't you even going to open it?" She said half-surprised.

"Later", was the reply. "I've got things to do."

"It's from Admissions," she said, half teasingly.

Artee hesitated, then glanced over his shoulder. "Big deal."

II

When the car engine started again, it never stopped during the next three hours, - only pausing once at a gas station. It was deaf to the mother's dogmatic plea to remain, the boy's fierce rebuttal, and blind to the mother's startled, indignant look as she saw her son walk out of the house. It was indifferent to the geographical transformations... the clustered houses, the rolling farmlands, the dense forests... insensitive to the change from pavement to gravel. To *it*, the northerly journey was only a smooth movement of oiled pistons and gears, of burning fuel and exhausts.

Tightening the straps of his backpack, Artee stood on a single car trail, the knee-length grass growing in the middle, spreading to the packed ground, as wide as car tires, and then to waist high green ferns. He eyed the mass of jack pines which surrounded his parked car, then turned and started walking on the sparse gravel and sand, noticing forests on either side; of more jack pines and scattered taller white pines, of oak, maple, and clustered whitish barked poplar—all growing from a waist high, green-ferned soil. After several minutes, the road suddenly climbed, and he spotted the small pothole containing the lone tamarack off to his left. He smiled.

While staring into the foliage, the adrenaline made his stomach churn. The path was overgrown and wild, yet because of the deer and animals, it still resisted the forest's inclination to absorb its winding passage. Smiling, he left the road and entered beneath the archway of tree branches, hearing a robin singing and a heat bug sounding its buzzing, high pitch trill.

Far in the growth, the forest floor once again began to slope upward; the trees and brush began to thin. Though tired, Artee increased his pace with added anticipation until the runway came suddenly onto an open knoll. He stopped. Below him lay a quiescent, small lake. Unknown by many—only an old logging trail on the other side allowed access by car—and then a door handle or dented fender was sometimes taken as an entrance fee by the large, close growing trees on each side of the secluded passage.

The sun was setting into the trees and reflected from the calm motion of the water. Its glaring, golden brilliance hurt Artee's eyes; he shaded them to admire the water's serenity and observe the surroundings. There was no one there. No one was fishing or camping. As hoped for, he was alone.

After setting up his tent on a grassy, level location, he unzipped the grocery section of his pack and pulled out a half-loaf of French bread and small jars of peanut butter and strawberry jam. With his Swiss army knife, he cut two slices of the bread, being careful not to crush it as he cut. He also spread the peanut butter as carefully as he could, protecting the soft texture of the bread, and the jam on the other, mating the two slices. He wrapped the remaining heel of the small loaf and returned it to his pack. He unscrewed the cap to his canteen and took a long swig of cool water. Excess ran down his chin and he turned his head sharply, wiping it on the shoulder of his cotton T-shirt. He looked at the sandwich discerningly and smiled before taking a monstrous bite out of it. He bit and swallowed as if a metal sheerer had been left cutting in the automatic position. He paused about halfway through and took another swallow of water before devouring the rest. Giving out a large belch, he got up and began to collect firewood.

Nearby, to the north of his tent, he noticed a sharp drop in the terrain and a huge, thick cedar swamp. Turning his back to the dense mass, he concentrated on scavenging the area farthest away from the darkening bog.

As he was pulling a rotted stump apart, a loud disturbance began ringing above him. First one, then another, and yet another. The air was suddenly filled with their cries, "Thief, thief, thief...."

Pausing, Artee spotted the flock of birds sitting, as if vultures, in a group of nearby trees. "Damn whiskeyjacks," he said in a whisper. Finding a stone, he hurled it at the birds with all his strength. The flock quickly scattered and disappeared, leaving the region peaceful again. Artee nodded his head triumphantly and continued picking up the half-decayed wood.

By this time, the sun had escaped the sky, but still its light showed from behind the trees, bursting upward, as if to begin another day. Seeing this, Artee promptly became satisfied with the pile he had collected, but before leaving it, gathered some dry lichen, small twigs, and scraped some dry pine sap off a tree, placing it all in the shape of a teepee in the center of a cleared area surrounded by a circle of large rocks. Without further delay, he went over to his tent to assemble his bamboo fly rod. Within a few minutes, he was with it at the lake's shore.

He lingered to observe the small, oblong body of water before casting. He could see long filaments of brownish weeds near the drop-off, amid patches of white-flowered lily pads. Beyond was the deep blue of the water, almost black in appearance. He found an open spot large enough to back-cast without getting into tree limbs or brush. Working his rod, he roll-cast the small red and white popper with a hula skirt out onto the mirror of water, just beyond the group of lily pads. The lure hit with a splash, the tiny waves moving out from it, as if to wrinkle the entire lake's surface. As it rested, Artee's eyes began absorbing other movements. Water striders were racing on invisible roads, their legs running as if on land. Below them, small mosquito larvae were twisting and turning, as if impatient of the world that they were in. Farther from shore, a gold sandy crater had been formed. A pair of bluegills wavered beside each other in its center.

Glancing across the lake, he noticed fog forming just above the water. He set his pole down on the ground and began walking around till he found a fat enough log to grab and drag down to the water. He laid it a few feet from the water and sat down on it. As he reached for his pole, a distant largemouth bass erupted from the water and inhaled the artificial lure attached to his slacked line. By the time he regained his senses and pulled back hard to set the hook, the fish had swallowed it, digested it, and excreted it whole back out into the water.

Artee pulled the dejected lure in, and casted once again. This time he watched, like a hawk watches a wandering field mouse. He raised his rod to move the lure toward him. The popper responded with a tempting "ker-plunk", but the only action was the diminishing waves created by the lure's movement.

He cast again and again, but without results. "They'll do it to you every time," he grumbled.

Throughout the attempts, he hadn't noticed what was approaching from behind. The frogs should have forewarned him. Or perhaps the bat, which flew over the lake, diving and rising for insects. But he hadn't taken notice. The lake was so attractive and illuminating. It wasn't until he felt the penetrating chill coming from the forest that he turned and noticed that the darkness of night had arrived. In one glimpse, Artee realized that he had never been totally alone in the woods before. No sounds of his sister or parents, no noise of the factory or its workers.

He stood at the water's edge and began to reel his line in. The more he looked into the forest, the more he heard, the more he saw what was not there. The forest was talking—but differently. Every sound had no face. Leaving the tranquil lake behind him, Artee started for his tent, the fireflies, like tiny blinking eyes, surrounding him.

First one thing, then another. Mosquitoes began flying thick as locusts, their buzzing insane. He was soon slapping his arms and neck to avoid their bites, even though they seldom landed. A gentle breeze made the leaves rustle. Staring in the direction of the sound, it seemed as if forms began to loom from the darkness; stumps, shrubs became creatures to his sight. The frogs bellowed forth mournfully from the swamp. From it, he swore a sinister beast was lurking. He swung his fishing pole viciously back and forth, as if to give warning.

Climbing the hill to his campsite, his feet slid in the quicksand-like earth. "Damn," he shouted, falling. He quickly got back up and continued his ascent until he finally arrived at his campsite. Somewhat relieved, he searched along the ground and found rocks, which he pried from the ground's grasp. Turning toward the swamp, he commenced to throw them, sending the hard mass of earth crashing noisily through the brush. When he could find no more, he stood, his chest heaving in the cool air. The frogs, which had become silent, were now croaking again as before.

Suddenly shafts of light cast themselves upon him. Looking up quickly, he saw the ball-like moon peeking over the eastern horizon. His lungs suddenly relaxed into a deep breath as his hands began to search through his pockets. Pulling them out, he revealed to the moonlight, his flint and steel.

He quickly crouched over and began to repeatedly strike the steel against the flint, trying to direct the sparks toward the small pile of twigs, lichen and sap. A small glow started, and he began to gently blow the ember, igniting it into a small flame. He carefully laid more twigs on it, the flame growing higher. He smiled as he heard the wood crackle. As his flames grew higher, he could see the shadow of himself—hunched over the pile of wood like an ape walking on all fours.

The fire made the night pull suddenly away, forcing it to stand at a distance. Soon he was adding more wood, the flames growing higher into the sky. The fire popped and hissed at him. He looked at the surrounding forest; the trees and brush were beginning to take on their regular appearance, but the swamp was yet dark, still breathing, still repelling.

He was able to see the ground clearly now and could detect more large rocks. Prying them out of the ground, he laid them, one on top of another near the tent. The column of rocks glistened from the firelight.

His breathing finally returned to normal. The young camper sat down to watch the glowing embers and dancing flames. The firelight built an immense protective wall around him as its warmth drove the heavy night air away. He enjoyed its heat, his face feeling hot and dry from the miniature sun.

Miles and miles away, across forests and countryside—far from the congenial sphere of the campfire—loomed the deserted factory, its inner recesses cloaked in an impenetrable vale of darkness. Except for the scurrying sound of an occasional rat running across a rusted pile of scrap steel, a morbid silence filled its stagnant air. Outside, the luminescent beams of a Mercury Vapor lamp guarded its entrance.

Its present condition, however, did not appear in the mind of the young outdoorsman, who sat mesmerized by the power of the blazing wood. Instead, past recollections of his meeting with the boss man precipitated in his mind, bringing a jovial mood, an air of exaltation.

"Well, looks like I'm finally going to make it," he said before the fire. "I should be able to operate the mills soon. Have a real job. No more degrading, scabby work for me. I'll bring in some big money, too. Get that apartment, buy all those things I need—a stereo, maybe a boat and motor, just like all my friends."

He paused after hearing his words. He could visualize the other workers, especially the fat foreman. "Why do I want to be like them?" he asked himself. "Crap," he said repulsively. He shrugged. "Well, I'll at least finally be able to be on my own."

Suddenly he got up and went to his tent. From the zippered pouch of his backpack, he pulled out a long, white envelope. As he slowly returned to the campfire, the blade of his Swiss Army knife carefully slit the seal open. By the intense flickering light, he pulled the letter out and noticed the first word, in capital letters, "CONGRATULATIONS". He scanned the rest of the words, with the visions of the mill factory alternating with the new building of the college he had visited several months ago. He sat down on a small section of a log, refolding the printed words and returning them into the envelope. He folded it in half and slid it into the front pocket of his shirt.

As the fire exploded a group of sparks into the air, he glanced up to see them drift leisurely away, till their glitter faded. He sat back as the smell of smoking, burning pine floated lazily from the little hill. The fire sputtered and crackled, sending more sparks into the air. He watched them as they were carried by the heat turbulence, till their glow was extinguished.

Beyond, he could see the lake shimmering in the night. The tops of trees made a smooth horizon around the water, but he could see on the far side the branches of a lone pine sharply standing out, high above the other trees. "Must be quite an old one," he said to himself. "I wonder why the lumberman left it there? Probably a White Pine." He glanced to his right and began to study the sky and its stars. He easily could see the Big Dipper, then the Little Dipper, thanks to his Boy Scout days. He followed the imaginary line from the Big Dipper to the handle of the Little. Polaris. His eyes then stared at the stars above him and the bright band of stars in the Milky Way. He contemplated its stealthy blackness and the hundreds, thousands, millions of sparkling orbs. Finally, after several minutes, his eyes followed the glittering streak until he could see the lone, tall pine tree. He stared blankly at it.

It was the sky. The huge, immense sky. He kept glancing up at it and wondering about its enormity and how he was just a speck in the universe, sitting there by his fire in northern Michigan – or it might as well have been in northern Atlantis as far as that went. He felt incredibly small, powerless, as if a pitiful particle of dust. The brief spirit of celebration surrounding his future prospects dissipated.

He released a heavy sigh as the fire continued crackling.

"Well, ole Artee."

He talked as if an invisible person were standing before him. His voice sounded serious and slightly remorseful.

"Now that ya got yourself back on the ground again, maybe you should really look at it." He paused and shook his head. "What ya going to do now with this life? With you?" He glanced up. "Look at that damn sky, would ya? So blasted big. I wonder how far it goes? Does it ever end? How did it come into existence anyway? When was *it's* beginning? I'm so insignificant," he muttered.

He could see the round, bright moon and the dark areas where craters were located. He sighed. "What are you going to do here? Live seventy years, then die? Make a bunch of money, then become the dust and dirt for other succeeding generations to walk on?" He reached over and unzipped a pouch on his pack and pulled out an apple. He also grabbed a canteen that was leaning up against the tent. Sitting back, he unscrewed the opening and took a few gulps, some of the water running down his neck.

"Yep. Shot right through since I was born. First, school, school, school. Be something they said. Make good for yourself. And me just stepping into that gun barrel and being fired. Just pushed right on through like everyone else. But now what? Do I continue on in school or do I start working and just travel right on till it stops or ends … and die?" He kept glancing up at the sky. He *was* talking to someone.

"Aw sure. I know. It's crazy. Why disturb it? Everyone is in that tube. School. Get a job. Marry. Have a home, raise kids. Get old. Become a grandfather. It's not all bad. Look at all the people before you – and the ones you know now. Had to be a good reason for it." He pulled some grass out of the ground and stuck a long one in his mouth. He began chewing on it. He leaned over and threw a small log on the fire. A cloud of sparks ascended into the crisp, cool, night air.

"But do you really want to start working—day in and day out—just for money and more things? Is that all life is? Money? Oh, I know. There's college, and I sure need to learn a lot more, but do you want to start all over—school, school, school?" He looked up to the sky and said earnestly, "But I want to do something important—for me—and for everyone – for this Earth. Not just exist and die!"

He spit the grass out and looked down to the lake. He talked far away.

"Boy, it's strange. I never really have considered it. Ever since I started work at the factory, it's just been thoughts of working, moving up, and making money. Not much else. But now, I guess I shouldn't count it out. At least not yet." He looked down at the ground. "I guess I just gotta do what I *can* do and go from there. Can do," he said again. "I wonder what I *can* do—and do well?" He looked at the apple while rotating it in his hands. "Maybe there's an orchard that I could work in?" He laughed and tossed it carelessly to the ground, no longer wanting to eat it.

He turned his head and saw the swamp staring. "Ya, I know. No common sense. It's hard enough to get any job anywhere nowadays. And you just gotta have a job. And it's better to stay where your friends are." He thought of his parents. "I know they want me to go to college, but…….I need money! I could always leave later, or else get an apartment or house; it's not so bad. It could be a lot worse. And if you stay, it sure would be a lot easier."

He looked up to the sky. The feeling returned. "But …" He cried out pleadingly, "*What do I do?*" His voice echoed across the lake and was swallowed by the silence. He pictured his parents, brothers and sister, and grandparents.

"Damn. Am I gutless? I keep saying I want to do something that no one else does. But it's always the same." He remembered Dafne. She too, was over, gone. He shook his head and looked into the fire, watching the flames lick themselves around the log. Long did he stare into the passive inferno, till his eyelids drooped with the penetrating heat. Yawning, he finally gave a quick glance around.

"Well," he said in a half stupor. "Guess it's no use now. Just a waste of time." He added one last huge oak log to the fire and stood up. He shouted to the lake.

"Who cares, anyways? And what does it matter?" He spat in the fire and heard it sizzle. Shaking his head, he crawled into the tent and got into his sleeping bag. He stared up into the darkness of the canvas and listened as a nearby whippoorwill began its call before falling into a deep sleep.

III

He heard a noise; his ears strained to hear it again. Then from far, far away, like a slow-moving wave, it began to flow toward him. First, like a whisper – as if the wind were sighing. Closer it approached, the sigh becoming more intense. His heart pounding. His mind—trying to send it back, trying in vain to eliminate it. Closer, up from the direction of the swamp, through the trees and brush. Artee's body rigid, tense, waiting. Now, it surrounding him. Then—silence. He saw the tent's flap as it hung motionless. "Get the hell out of here!" he yelled.

Suddenly the sound began to fill his ears, now pulsating—beating. Then a hand—a hair thickened hand—grabbed the tent's flap and slowly pulled it open, revealing a Gorgonian face concealed by frizzled black hair with a huge bulging forehead, and eyes which seemed to stare magnetically into his. Him—propped up in the sleeping bag, his hand trying to move to the black sheath, but could not. Trying to yell, but could not. It watching him, as if not able to understand the terror. The look in its eyes, empty, searching. Now extending its wrinkled hand, its calloused palms stretched out, as if to receive or offer something. The hand trembling.

Looking horrified at the quivering palm, Artee made one last desperate attempt to free himself. In a panic frenzy, the chains suddenly broke; there was a swift movement unmistakably to the black sheath and straight toward the chest of the creature, the golden blade flashing as it arched forward. The yielding creature falling back; the young person on top of it, thrusting, jabbing madly; crying out with each lunging strike. The forest echoing his cries until finally he recognized the discerning eyes of its face. Then in disbelief, he pulled the knife out, dropped it to the ground, and recoiled violently backward. The hideous creature was motionless, but its body and face were changing, losing its hair, the protruding forehead receding.

Pulling the sleeping bag in front of him, the young man cried out in agony. "No…no…" The face changing … changing …

Artee sat up, the perspiration running from his forehead, his hands wet with sweat, his eyes searching the inside of the dimly lit tent. He looked at the lifeless objects with a peculiarity, constantly recalling the last visage of the creature. His eyes focused on the doorway flap, not sure what he would find on the other side. As he recognized the faint glimmering of sunlight filtering through the canvas, his tense body began to relax. He investigated further, finding his sheathed knife beneath his pillow, the blade clean. Glancing around the inside of the tent once more, he laid back and laughed nervously to himself, shaking his head back and forth.

The light coming through the canvas gave a sense of evening outside, but Artee could tell by the myriad sound of songbirds that it was morning. Silently he began to get dressed, becoming more and more unconcerned about the elapsed episode with the apparition. As he pulled his T-shirt over his head, he felt the curls of his long hair.

"Time to go," he said to himself. Pulling the t-shirt back over his head, he got his swiss army knife out, and a small mirror from his backpack. Propping it up near the entrance, he opened the small scissors and began to carefully cut his hair above his ears.

"Not bad," he said while scrutinizing himself in the mirror. "I'll get it trimmed later."

He continued getting dressed, and was pulling his boots on, thinking of fishing for some early morning bass, when he heard a sound outside the tent. He listened breathlessly and soon recognized it as a digging or scraping of the ground. He then could hear a snorting and sniffing of some animal. He shrugged his shoulders and smiled. Skunk? Coon? A bear? Quietly he crept to the tent's opening on his hands and knees and peered through it, immediately seeing the animal.

Through the smoke and white-ash covered embers of the fire, in the dim light of morning, stood a huge dog, its head bowed to the ground, its snout burrowing through dirt while one of its mighty front paws sporadically tore at a mat of leaves and decaying vegetation as it held the other paw up, tucked beneath its silver coat that was tightly stretched upon its ribs. There were burrs and broken thorns tangled into its fur, a bent porcupine quill stuck into the side of its face, and Artee could see a large quill stuck in the up-held paw. Its size and color suggested that it was a wolf, but as far as Artee knew, wolves had disappeared from the area long before he was born.

Silently, Artee moved his hand. The dog suddenly froze, looking suspiciously at the tent. The smoke from the campfire altered and distorted all perceptions. It seemed as if the young man was crawling no longer from a tent, but a cave. His outstretched hand was beckoning for the animal to come toward him. Ten thousand years seemed to transcend between them, like the mists of the fire.

The dog turned and hobbled on its three legs, keeping the fourth forepaw bent beneath it. Artee instantly responded, in a beseeching, yet calm plea, "Come on boy, it's okay. Come on, I'm not going to hurt you. Come on."

It was his quiet tone. The dog's ears perked up; it stopped and turned again toward the human, still holding its forepaw from the ground.

Artee crawled on his hands and knees slowly toward the dog, constantly reassuring it, their eyes fixed upon each other. The dog remained motionless until Artee's hand moved toward the paw.

The dog bolted into the edge of the tall ferns and trees.

Again, Artee called out, "It's okay! It's okay!"

The dog stopped again.

Artee turned and crawled back to his tent. He opened the side pocket on his backpack and pulled out the remains of the French loaf of bread. He crawled back toward the dog, with a chunk of bread held in his one outstretched hand.

"Come on boy, it's okay," reassured the young man. He held the bread out toward the dog.

It sniffed the air and hobbled toward him cautiously. Approaching the hand, it took a monstrous bite and swallowed the entire piece.

"That a boy," Artee reassured. "That a boy."

Artee's upheld palm continued until it contacted beneath the dog's chin. He began to scratch the dog while talking soothingly.

The dog's eyes looked straight into Artee's.

Artee continued to scratch its throat while looking at the invested paw with the large quill.

"This is going to hurt like hell," he said half sympathetically. His hand left the dog's throat and went down to take hold of the dog's ankle. He held it gently but firmly while the other hand slowly moved to the arrow-like quill. He glanced up to the dog's eyes.

"Ready?" he asked.

He grabbed the quill and yanked hard. The dog screamed in pain and pulled away from the human, leaving the quill with Artee.

In a few mighty bounds, the dog soon disappeared toward the swamp.

The young man was up instantly, his legs carrying him after the fleeing animal. He was whistling, calling him to come back, running in the direction that he had seen him last; running blindly into the mass of cedar and brush, surrounded now by the bog and a tangling web of branches.

His voice was echoing into the swamp as he ran into a bottomless quagmire of black muck and water. He was already sunk to his knees as he began to wrestle with the sucking force beneath his thighs. He dove back to the bank of cedar trees. His hands grabbed the solid ground, his fingers digging into the fine network of roots, his arms pulling him frantically from the grasp of the mire. Wiggling and twisting his way out of the ooze, he finally succeeded in gaining the safety of the damp moss. Getting up, he strained to see through the brush.

He called out one more time. There were no sounds, nor any sign of movement.

"A dog. A dog," he kept repeating in half-belief as he turned and began to retrace his chaotic trail through the swamp. He continued to look over his shoulder as he climbed the sloping hill back to his tent.

Standing by the dwindling fire, he watched the smoke rise silently, swirling straight into the air. He looked down into the white ashes and the black charred remains of the wood. There were no flames, only gray smoke. A gentle breeze suddenly came up, causing the smoke to change its direction. It blew into his face, stinging his eyes, blinding him momentarily. He stumbled around to the other side of the fire, his eyes watering as he tried to rub-out the smoke. When he opened them, blinking till light came into focus, he was facing the lake.

The waters were calm, smooth and shiny, as if covered by a thin sheet of ice. There was an orange glare dancing on its surface. He could hear birds singing, not just chirping, but singing—flawlessly clear. The robin's notes came to him first, its varying melody penetrating sharp and distinct. Then other birds blended their notes with the robins'—warblers, chickadees, a cardinal—a multitude of separate songs intermingling, interwoven into one.

He smelled the remains of the campfire as it mixed with the other indescribable odors; of pine, cedar, decayed leaves, and syringa. He looked out into the coniferous forest and oak and maple, of poplar, dogwood, and cherry laurel and took a deep breath of the cool refreshing air.

With the sun shining on him, the mud from the swamp began to dry hard on his pants and boots. Suddenly, across the lake, piercing through the dense growth of the forest came a low and mournful howl. The forest air became silent. The crying howl of a dog repeated itself; each time, the sonorous tone more penetrating, stronger than the preceding one, as if a huge church bell were being struck with added fervor. After another echoing cry, it ceased. Artee searched across the lake and it seemed that for one brief moment, he could see him again, running through the forest: a glimpse.

There was a momentary pause, as if the surrounding life was listening, then once again the birds were singing, and the sounds were restored.

The sun was climbing. Artee looked at his watch; the sweep-hand ticked loudly on his wrist. Taking it off, he put it into his pocket. He contemplated the recent events, looking in the direction where he had last seen the dog. His eyes wandered to the lake. A smile slowly formed across his face.

Taking his fishing pole, he tied a hook at the end of the line. Above the hook, he bit a split shot around the monofilament. As he walked down to the water, he overturned rotting logs and decayed, moist leaves till he found a live, wiggling earthworm. He baited it, threading the tip of the hook above the collar and into the body of the worm. It curled and wound itself around the shank. As he approached the water, he counted 7 luminous white swans on the far shore, their outstretched heads like beacons. They were singing, their melodious voices directed toward him. Artee glanced over and found an opening between trees, where he half-casted his bait onto the water. The worm and lead weight splashed together and sank to the bottom. Laying the pole down, he crawled onto a huge boulder at the shore's edge. Stretching out onto his belly, he raised his head and saw the tall tree across the lake with its top glistening in sunshine. The swans were directly below it at the water's edge, still singing. He looked down and dipped his hands into the cold water, splashing it over his face. His eyes opened wide, he reached for his pole and sat on the boulder holding it and the taut line as the water dripped from his face.

About a hundred yards away, he watched a crane motionlessly stalk its prey. Soon he saw it spear its long bill swiftly in the water and raise it into the air with a twisting fish. Beyond, on the shore, unaware of human presence, a deer came and drank from the pond.

The fisherman let the worm sit on the bottom till the sun made him unbutton his flannel shirt. He never moved his pole. He kept visualizing that a bass was just about ready to take the bait. He didn't want to frighten or disturb anything, so he just left the worm where he had placed it.

When he finally saw the line move through the water, he held the pole tight. He allowed it to run with the bait till it began to slow, and then he set the hook hard. The water exploded. A large bass thrashed to free itself. His pole bent double; the fish dove and jumped and dove again. His drag started its high-pitch *zizz* as the fish swam for deeper water.

Artee kept the pole high, letting the fish struggle with the added resistance. He stopped its initial run and started to retrieve the huge mass, but it turned and took the line out again. This continued, back and forth, for nearly thirty minutes; the fish taking line out, the young fisherman reeling it back in.

Artee's arms and shoulders were aching, but he could see that the fish's runs were getting shorter. By keeping a near-break tension on the line, he pumped back with his pole and saw the fish turn toward the shore. He kept the unrelenting tension on it, and slowly reeled the line in. Unable to gather further strength, the fish gradually ceased its struggle and was finally beached.

Artee worked his thumb into its mouth and lifted it up by the lower jaw. The bass flopped against his arm. He noticed how the sunlight reflected off its wet, shiny scales as its enormous gills were breathing the drying, deadly air. Its eyes seemed to look at everything. Artee worked the hook free and held the fish out in front of him, beholding the swollen belly full of spawn. Again, its heavy weight flopped against his arm as he slowly lowered it back into the water.

At first it never reacted, only its gills slowly moved. Artee was concerned that it was dead and bent down closer to see it. Suddenly with a mighty thrust of its tail, the fish sent water splashing over the fisherman and swam unharmed into the depths. Smiling, Artee watched as it swam away, the biggest fish he had ever caught.

He stood staring over the waters—the surface calm again. The sun was tall in the sky, moving. He looked back to his tent. Taking his pole, he made the climb back up the hill.

As the young man was taking down his tent, he found the pile of hair that he had cut off. Gathering it up, he laid it at the base of the stone column that was still standing.

"Thanks for protecting me," he said. Looking over toward the swamp, he found the apple that he had carelessly thrown to the ground the night before. After briefly inspecting it to see only a bruise, he casually ate it while preparing his pack.

It was nearly noon when he had his equipment strapped to his back. He knew if he stayed longer, he'd be dealing with the huge traffic jams on the way back. As he tossed the apple-core into the swamp, thoughts of the dog, of school, and his job briefly came to him. He spoke ruefully, "Ah well. Maybe someday. Maybe things will just happen to me, maybe it's destined. Or maybe someday I'll get up enough nerve and do it myself.

Surprise everybody. Sure," he said more optimistically. "One of these days. But right now, I just need a little more time."

Standing on the hill, he glanced at the surroundings for a final view. His eyes came to rest on the surface of the lake. Quiet, peaceful, blue and clear. Suddenly he heard a thunder growing louder and louder. A low flying jet screamed by and was gone. Far off in the distance, he could hear the rumble of a diesel truck engine as it downshifted on a hill of a highway. The water of the pond sparkled.

The train. The train. So small against the forest. But he had seen its strength. Its power. Standing there at the pond, he understood its churning wheels and the whistle. He knew its curse. Slow, steady, engulfing, spreading across the land like a disease. It... growing larger and larger, bellowing its black smoke, shaking the ground, going faster and faster. The people climbing madly on board, shoveling the wood, the coal, in its belching, fuming hungry mouth. "Gotta keep it going. Can't stop it now." Tearing through this land; no brains, just speed and strength and power. Whistles blowing, bells ringing, people cheering, waving their hands out the windows.

Artee turned away from the small body of water and walked slowly through the woods, listening to the birds singing, smelling the strong scent of pine, feeling the ferns and earth crunch beneath his feet. Back he walked through the forest of overhanging tree branches; the sun blistering straight down upon him. Coming out to the dirt road and the waiting automobile.

He did not hesitate. Upon packing the car, he took a deep breath and started the engine. The car backed out onto the road and left the forest in a stream of dust.

Soon he approached the highway. He stopped before entering and noticed that there were many high steel poles carrying power lines that ran parallel with the road. They went as far as he could see.

He had to wait, the traffic was already heavy. His tires screeched onto the pavement; he was now part of the long formation of moving cars. He followed along, driving at the speed limit.

The people behind were tailgating, causing Artee to increase his speed.

The flow of cars moved onward, through the hilly farmland and small towns, moving farther south, closer to the larger cities.

Suddenly Artee saw a dog bolt across the road. A car struck it just before it reached the other side, sending it tumbling onto the gravel of the roadside. He heard a distant agonizing cry. Artee never saw brake lights, but he slammed on his and eased his vehicle onto the road's shoulder. The other cars continued, uninterrupted. Ahead, the body of the dog was stretched out on the gravel, its front paws and head resting on scattered patches of dry grass. It lay motionless, the wind blowing across its long golden hair, blowing across a field of green grass and brilliant, purple-flowered fireweed.

Artee threw open his car door and got out. He ran to the dog, but just as he lowered himself to it, he slowed his movements. Carefully he touched the rear paw of the animal. There was no response. He called out, "Come on, boy, get up," but it remained motionless.

Artee laid his hands on the warm body and gently shook it. "Come on, you can make it! Come on!"

The dog lay still. There was bright red blood oozing from the dog's mouth. Artee ran his fingers through the long yellow hair. "Oh God!" Artee cried out. "Oh God!" The only thing he could hear was the passing of one car after another as he watched the motionless dog before him.

He checked for a collar. Nothing. He glanced around. There were no houses anywhere, no people.

The young man got up and returned to his car where he opened his trunk. "Damn cars," he muttered to himself. "I've got to get rid of this thing, give it back to my parents, and go back to riding my bike, or something." He pushed some of his things—the tent and backpack – off to the side and spread some old newspapers on its bottom. As the line of cars continued to pass by, he went over and carefully lifted the animal and carried it back to the car where he laid it on the newspapers and slammed his trunk.

The traffic was becoming more congested. No one would allow him back onto the road. Finally, he pulled out and forced his way between two cars, making a U-turn. A sound of screeching tires could be heard. Driving on, Artee could see the driver's finger flashing out his window and hear some of his universal language.

There were no cars on the northbound lane of the highway. In his mirror, he could still see the line-up of tail lights.

The migratory journey over pavement, onto gravel, past towns, into forests—elapsed without relationship to time, as if time itself was suspended. Indeed, since the driver's thoughts were undergoing such vigorous activity, it seemed as if the destination was reached within a blink of an eye.

Listening to several robins singing, Artee noticed the trees, the lake, and the sky as he stood in the small clearing. With the dog lying on a rectangular shaped area of flattened grass, the laborer fell onto his knees and started digging with his hands. The hard ground cut his fingers till blood seeped from them, yet he persisted, finally using the gold blade of his knife to loosen the ground and his hands to scoop the sandy soil out, till the hole was several feet deep. Then he placed the dog gently in, as a few beads of sweat dripped from his forehead and fell into the grave.

He paused to observe the dog as it lay in the ground, its long, golden hair motionless.

"You'll need something for your journey." He reached into his pocket and pulled out the new, shiny coin.

Artee reached down and placed the silver piece over the blood-caked lips of the animal. The eagle stared up at him.

"I'll see you on the other side, someday", he said.

Carefully spreading the dirt back into the hole, Artee watched the animal as it disappeared. He then got up, found a large, smooth, round whitish rock, and placed it gently on the scarcely bulging mound of dirt. Stepping back, he stood quietly.

"It's the best I could do."

Suddenly a strong gust of wind whistled through the trees. Raising his head, Artee stared toward the direction of the lake, to the west, where the sun was now shining. Not far from him stood the silver dog.

As the wind continued to whip the trees back and forth, Artee spoke clearly, "I wish I could stay here. With *you*. But I can't. After all these years, all these years," he said slowly and loudly. "I have much to do."

The dog lowered itself onto the ground, its forepaws stretched out in front of it, as if bowing to the mortal. Raising its head, it watched the strange being walk through the brush until gone from sight.

THE END

www.ingramcontent.com/pod-product-compliance
Lightning Source LLC
LaVergne TN
LVHW011843060526
838200LV00054B/4144